HEA

The Hair-Raising Sequel to BELLYACHE

by
CRYSTAL MARCOS

Cat Marcs Publishing
Silverdale, Washington

Cat Marcs Publishing
PO Box 54
Silverdale, WA 98383

www.CatMarcs.com

Printed in the United States of America

ISBN 978-0-9843899-1-9
LCCN 2012933129

For my little cupcake

Praise for Crystal Marcos's
BELLYACHE
A Delicious Tale

"The author is talented and imaginative. This is a delightful tale sure to please elementary age students. I eagerly await the next offering by this author."

— *Readers Favorite*

"'Bellyache' is a choice read for younger readers just getting ready to move onto chapter books."

— *Midwest Book Review*

"Crystal Marcos provides a moving tale to help us learn to forgive, no matter how hard it is. Although this is her first book, she displays through it her startling ability to teach a difficult matter in a fun and appealing way that children will understand. Kids will want to read this book over and over again!"

— Cecilia Lee, *Allbook Reviews*

Winner of a 2011 *Readers Favorite* Silver Award

Contents

HEADACHE

Back at the Sweet Shop

Darkness.

"Where are we?" Joe asked.

"Shhh, I think I hear voices. Don't move," Angela replied.

"I don't hear anything."

"Me neither," Angela agreed.

"Follow that light," Joe advised.

"Hey! That is my nose!" Angela wailed.

"Get off my toe, please!"

"Yuck, I stuck my finger in something sticky!" Angela griped, and then banged into something hard. "Ouch, I think I just found the door!"

"Hurry, open it!" Joe replied.

"I am," Angela said.

A relaxed smile spread across her face as she met Joe's eyes. She glanced past his head and instantly her smile became a look of horror, followed by a scream. As she instinctively covered her mouth with her hands, smearing the white sticky substance across her nose, she screamed again.

"What is it?" Joe said shakily, not moving his eyes from hers.

"Get it off my face, get it off my face!" Angela finally screeched, her arms fanning at her nose which was covered in whipped cream frosting.

Joe sprang into action, grabbing a dish rag. He worked briskly to remove the unwanted substance. When not a trace was left, he said, "It's all gone."

She didn't reply and stared past him with a look of fright.

Joe reluctantly turned to look over his shoulder. With terror upon him, he saw one single cupcake perched in the doorway staring at him. He glanced to the side of the door and saw a light switch. He switched it on.

Both children gasped. There was an excellent reason for their fright. Angela and Joe were Candonite children. Candonites were sweets and there were many different races. Angela was a cookie Candonite and Joe was a lemon-drop Candonite. Before them was a large walk-in refrigerator holding hundreds of miniature versions of themselves and people from their land. Cupcakes, fudges, brownies, chocolates, and other tasty treats lined the shelves. Many had fallen to the floor. Neither child spoke for several moments.

"I don't think we are in Maple Town any more. I don't think we are anywhere near it," Joe said.

"Obviously! This isn't our home!" Angela scoffed.

"Calm down!" Joe said. "Let's see if we can figure out what happened."

They both were very nervous, realizing they

were far from their own world, far from safety. They scanned the room which was now illuminated by the refrigerator lights. It was a kitchen.

"See what *you* have done?" Angela whined.

"Now you wait just a minute!" Joe said. "What do you mean, 'what *I* have done?'"

"Don't you remember? Peter and Lina had just saved us from that horrible Goaltan and the other Peblars." She shook her head as she tried to forget the awful time that the four of them spent escaping from Goaltan's dreadful lair. Thank goodness Peter and Lina came to their rescue. Otherwise, Joe and Angela would still be in Goaltan's freezing, putrid castle. Angela shook her head harder, as if to shake the memory right out of her head and continued. "We were standing in front of the special delivery box that brought Peter and Lina from their world to Maple Town. They were on their way home. You reached out to bid Peter farewell with a pat on his back. I knew that wasn't a good idea. I grabbed at your hand to try to stop you while they were saying the magic words to bring them home and—poof—here we are!"

"So you think we are in Peter's world, Earth?" Joe asked.

"Yep," Angela replied with a frown.

"I didn't know this would happen; there is no use in blaming anyone. We should use our energy trying to figure out how to get back home," Joe said calmly.

"And just how do you propose that? Should

we jump in this mixing bowl and be on our way?" she said sarcastically.

"Angela, calm down," Joe replied.

"Don't tell me to calm down! I don't know anything about this place except that they eat things that resemble us. Look at those poor miniature Joes stacked against the wall!"

Joe examined bags of lemon drops encased in their plastic tombs. He was horrified.

"And I am sure there are some positively helpless cookies with rainbow chips, resembling me, lying around here somewhere! I couldn't bear to see that."

"It will be all right," Joe reassured her. "Now let's take a look around so we can find out at least where we are."

They scanned the room and saw three doors. One was open, while the other two were closed. They decided on the open door to the left.

Joe reached around and felt for a light switch. They released sighs of relief when they saw it was plainly an office, with nothing to be afraid of. Once inside, they saw a picture of an older human man with glasses on the edge of his nose. He was standing in front of a building. The building sign read "Papa's Sweet Shop." They made their way around the small room, which was cluttered with papers, file cabinets, and baking books. In the back of the room was a wooden desk with a worn leather chair. A piece of duct tape was placed snugly on one arm. Another picture sat on the desk. The same man they saw in the other picture stood next to a woman about the same age and a smiling young boy.

"Peter!" the Candonite children shouted in unison. He looked a few years younger in the picture, but there was no mistaking him.

"This must be Peter's grandfather and grand-mother," Angela said.

"Great! At least we aren't too off base. We will be home in no time," Joe said, relieved. "There should be something here that can lead us to him."

They rummaged through papers and flipped open books with handwritten notes in them without any luck. Joe began opening drawers. He reached into one drawer when a bottle caught his eye. "Imported from Indonesia," its label read. He repeated the words aloud, wondering where on Earth Indonesia was. He adjusted the bottle so he could see its contents. Immediately he dropped it into the drawer and covered it up with a piece of paper before Angela could see that it contained quite beautiful rainbow chips. The middle drawer contained what they were hoping to find, an overstuffed Rolodex filled with addresses and phone numbers. Joe took it out and thumbed through it.

"Farmer...Fellows...Finney's Market...Come on Fis....Here it is, Fischer! Peter and Tracy Fischer." Joe was so excited at his find that he tore the card right out of the Rolodex. "Oops! I will give this back later," he said. He smiled at Angela who was clapping her hands gleefully, her colorful chips shaking as she did.

"713 Mulberry Place. This is where we go," Joe said.

"Do you think there may be a map around here somewhere?" Angela asked.

"It won't hurt to look," Joe answered.

Angela and Joe searched the desk drawers and looked in the file cabinet. After a few minutes, they found a town map. Joe wrote the house number on the edge of the map, circled Peter's neighborhood, and left the address card on the table. The Candonite children gave each other a quick hug and headed back to the kitchen. There were two doors they hadn't opened. They went to the nearer one, opening it cautiously and becoming more alert when they smelled the sweet scent of fresh-baked goods. Their bodies stiffened when they looked into the room, faintly lit by the fading sun. It was as though Angela and Joe were looking at a miniature version of their world. Only this version lay on plates and in jars and on shelves with prices for their lives displayed. The Candonite children were disgusted.

"I could never get used to this!" Angela hissed.

"You won't have to. We will be out of here and safe at home in no time," Joe reassured her.

A figure passed the window walking briskly and the children froze.

"Maybe we should wait until dark before venturing out to find Peter. We don't know if everyone will be as friendly as he is. Besides, we don't exactly blend right in, you know," Angela suggested. Joe agreed as he looked around again at the mini-Candonite graveyard.

"Let's make ourselves less conspicuous," he said. "Maybe there's something we can use to disguise ourselves."

A Barking Mess

"We have to be careful not to be seen," Joe said. "I am not so sure our disguises will fool anyone."

"I think we did a pretty good job with what we could find," Angela replied, straightening the apron she had placed over her head. She found it hanging on a hook in the kitchen and mistakenly thought it was a hat. She had tied a bow with the ties on the back of the apron on her head and the rest of the apron cascaded down the back of her neck and sides of her head. In addition, Angela wore a dress she made out of a pastel floral tablecloth she discovered in a cabinet. She held it together with safety pins she found in a drawer. Angela thought she looked splendid.

Joe felt awkward in his disguise despite Angela's encouragement. He found Papa's black fedora hat and a charcoal floor-length trench coat hanging in the office. He also tried on a spare pair of glasses Papa kept in a desk drawer. Surprisingly, after a minute of adjusting Joe could see out them perfectly fine. They were an exact fit and didn't dangle off his nose the way they did for Papa.

"We should stay in the shadows as much as

possible," Joe said.

Angela agreed.

"It may take us all night to get there," Joe added, gazing at the map.

"After we spent most of the day in Goaltan's ghastly castle and escaping, I hope I have the energy to stay awake," Angela said.

The Candonite children reflected on the day's events. Waking up that morning, Angela and Joe had had no clue they would end up in two different unknown worlds. They certainly didn't think they would have to be rescued twice in order to return home.

Angela and Joe stood near the glass window of the shop, taking note of the darkened streets, nothing like the shiny colorful ones back home. Joe began opening the door to start their quest when bright lights appeared in the distance. He quickly let go of the door and retreated inside. Soon they saw that the bright lights were connected to a car. But this car didn't hover off the ground like the ones back home.

"Interesting," Joe said.

"I'll say," Angela replied.

"Let's try this again," Joe said, reaching for the door.

As Joe and Angela exited Papa's Sweet Shop, they took note of the building number and approached the street sign on the corner. It read "Winters Road."

"The air is unpleasant here. It doesn't smell anything like home." Angela grimaced. It was another clue they were far away from the sweet smell of Maple Town.

The children traveled unnoticed for about an hour with one wrong turn. After rounding a corner, they were spotted by an elderly man. The man was just a few feet away walking briskly toward them. There was no time to react before he was upon them. He wore thick glasses and his silver hair hung long against his neck, his broad smile beaming at them.

He paused and spoke, "Top of the evening to you. Usually don't see many folk out this late. Doing my evening rounds. Not much of a sleeper myself."

Angela and Joe looked at each other in surprise and replied, "Evening."

"Doc says I shouldn't be out walking this late with my sight going and all. He worries about me running into trouble. I told him, I been walking these streets for 67 years and I ain't planning on stopping anytime soon. I ain't never been much of a sleeper. That's a nice hat you got there."

"Um, thanks," Angela replied.

"Well, I better be going. I got another four blocks to go before I get home. By the way, young man, yellow is a good color on you. Evening." The man nodded and hurried off.

"Evening," the children called after him. He waved back without turning around.

Angela and Joe looked at each other and let

out soft nervous giggles. They had obviously fooled the old man and were relieved they did.

Angela and Joe continued their traveling for quite some time, ducking in and out of alleys, narrowly missing being spotted by a passing taxi driver, when they heard the pattering of little feet behind them. When they swung around to investigate, they saw a pair of eyes and a long wagging tongue attached to a fuzzy little creature.

"What is that thing?" Angela shrieked, stepping back.

"Shoo! Go away!" Joe commanded. But the fuzzy little creature started wagging its tail.

"It's a dog!" Angela said. The dog peeked over his shoulder, and soon another identical dog slightly larger than the first appeared from the dark street.

"Not more of them," Joe said. Waving his arms, he gestured and said, "Shoo. Go on! Get!" No sooner did he have the words out of his mouth than two more dogs, one black and one dingy white, joined the others. All of them wagged their tails.

"Oh no!" Angela sighed.

With a flash of an eye the dogs sprinted toward the children, sniffing and licking at Joe and Angela's legs.

"Yuck!" Angela said as she tried to weave away from the dogs.

"They like the way we smell. We have to find a way to get them to leave us alone quickly before we wake someone," Joe said.

"I have an idea," Angela said. "Follow me." She turned around, heading toward the way they came, and began walking quickly. Joe did as he was told. It was difficult to walk with the dogs at their heels. Angela tripped over the smallest dog and it instinctively licked her face. She couldn't help it, she giggled. Joe helped her up. "There," she said, pointing at a dumpster in a seemingly lifeless faintly lit alley.

Joe jogged over with the dogs following closely behind, climbed on a crate, and peeked in. "Uh uh, no way," he said as he scanned the unwanted waste. "Sick! Don't humans know about recycling?"

"You got a better idea? We don't have time for this. Jump in," she coaxed.

Joe didn't budge. Angela pushed another crate beside the first, climbed up, and grabbed Joe's arm, pulling him in with her as she plunged into the heap of trash. The dogs barked after them.

"Did you really have to do that?" Joe whined.

"Yes," Angela answered. "Now roll around in it and cover up your natural smell." She demonstrated what she wanted.

"Disgusting!" said Joe as Angela rubbed an old rotting cabbage head against her body.

"Oh, lighten up," she said, as she grabbed a damp wet sponge and threw it at him. Joe said nothing and returned the favor, slinging a handful of something slimy and bright yellow across her shoulder. Angela gave him a "how dare you" look, followed by a giggle and began chucking trash at him left and right. Soon it was an all-out war. After a minute, Angela and Joe were crouching in opposite corners, covered from head to toe in waste.

Joe stated the obvious. "We may have over-done it."

"I think so." Angela looked Joe up and down and then at herself.

"I don't hear the dogs anymore," Joe said. He pulled himself up and peered out. He found the dogs staring back, their tails no longer wagging.

Angela joined him and they helped each other out of the dumpster, pushing and pulling. The dogs remained there, eyes fixed with blank faces. The little one was positioned in front. The dog's lip began to curl, a low soft growl came out, and he promptly turned and trotted away. The other dogs followed him.

"It worked!" Joe said. "You were right."

"And you doubted me," Angela said, feeling smug.

"Never again. But now we are terribly disgusting!" He laughed.

"Well, I like to think it was better than having those dogs lick us silly," Angela said.

"Hopefully, we can find something to clean some of this off," Joe said as a drop of goo dripped off the end of his nose.

"Is the map okay?" Angela asked.

Joe wiped his hand off on the crate and

reached into grandpa's coat pocket. "Looks good."

"Phew!" Angela whispered.

The Candonite children were soon back en route to Peter's.

"We smell REALLY bad," Angela said.

"I know. We have to do something about this," Joe replied.

A moment later Angela and Joe spotted a large gray cloth covering something in a driveway. They looked at each other. Without a word they knew what the other was thinking and moved slowly toward the driveway.

Joe stood guard while Angela removed the cover and discovered a beautiful white car underneath. She hurriedly wiped herself down, being careful to use the outside of the cloth. She didn't want to get anything on the spotless car. Joe went next, while Angela stood guard. He was just as careful. They put the cover neatly back on the car, then took a step back and examined their work. The cloth was no longer dull gray, but a kaleidoscope of colors.

As they walked away from the scene, Angela moaned, "I am beyond hungry."

"I could use something to eat myself."

"If you want me to keep walking, we are going to have to find something to eat," she told him.

Finally There

Crouching, Angela and Joe chowed down. They were in paradise. They had found a garden behind a fence in someone's back yard. The fence was low enough to simply step right over. There was luscious lettuce and marvelous green beans. It was their version of the sweet shop delights. Eating all those vegetables was like eating cakes and pies to them. There were other vegetables too, but they decided to leave those alone. Angela and Joe didn't want to take more than what was necessary to hold them over, until they could find some substantial food.

After eating, they rested for a moment in the tranquil garden before deciding it was time to get going. Joe pulled out the map and realized it wasn't too much further now.

"Almost there?" Angela asked when she saw a relaxed smile on Joe's face.

"Yes."

"Good, because the sun is starting to rise," Angela remarked. At that moment, they heard a car start nearby. Joe and Angela remained very still until they heard it drive off.

They traveled the rest of the way in total

stealth mode, super-fast and sneaky. Within minutes they were at Peter's house. It was at the corner of a cul-de-sac in a nice neighborhood. The lights were on. Someone was up.

"What now?" Joe asked. "We can't very well just go to the door, can we?"

A moment of silence passed and the garage doors opened. Angela and Joe ducked behind a car parked on the side of the road. It was Peter's dad leaving for work. He was tall, thin, dressed in a navy blue blazer with a crisp white collared shirt, and he carried a tan leather briefcase. He entered the SUV parked in the garage and drove off. The garage door shut. Joe and Angela ran over to a row of thick bushes against a fence in Peter's yard and wedged themselves in. No one could see them there.

A half hour later, Peter ran out the door. He headed to the car on the side of the road. His mother parked it there last night because Papa had parked crooked when he had taken him home the night before. His mother unlocked the doors from the driveway to let Peter in the car and she soon slid into the front driver seat.

"Well, what do we do now?" Angela whispered.

"I don't know. It looks as though Peter is going to school. He may be a while," Joe whispered back.

"We can't stay squished in these bushes all day," Angela whined.

"Then what do you suggest?" Joe asked.

Angela peeked out from the bushes and

scanned the area. "Let's get in there." She pointed toward an old boat at the side of the house. It looked as though it had been sitting there for quite some time. Joe agreed and they found their temporary new home in the dirty old boat. It was better than being squished up against the fence with branches in their ears and they could get some much-needed rest.

Easy Breezy Ham and Cheesy

"Peter is back," Angela said several hours later, peering out of the boat.

"Good. I was getting tired of playing thumb wars," Joe said. "My thumbs are sore."

Peter got out of the car and handed Mrs. Fischer his backpack. She went in the house and Peter walked down the driveway toward the cul-de-sac.

"Where is he going?" Angela gasped.

Peter stepped onto the sidewalk. He veered left and opened the mailbox. He muttered to himself, "I can't believe she doesn't believe me. I am ten now. I have grown up a lot since last year."

He headed back toward the house and was glad that his best friend Lina was coming over for dinner. *Then they will see, and then they will know I am telling the truth,* he thought. His family had chalked up his adventure in Maple Town as a result of his overeating, which led to a wildly vivid dream. Peter knew the truth and so did Lina. It was not a dream.

Peter heard his name as he approached the doorstep. It was a low call, a familiar voice. He walked toward the boat, where he found Joe and

Angela hiding. Peter couldn't believe it. They looked so relieved to see him.

"What are you guys doing here? How did you get here?" Peter asked astounded, as he climbed in the boat. "And what are you wearing?"

Angela and Joe told their story to Peter in a quick version. They knew Peter's mother was inside and didn't want her to come outside and cause a scene if she saw them.

"We need to get you guys inside," Peter said anxiously. "Now my mom will see that Candonites are real!"

"Are you sure that is a good idea, Peter?" Angela questioned.

"You two can't stay out here forever and besides you have less of a chance of being seen if you are actually indoors. Also, you should get cleaned up. You smell awful!" Peter said. Peter understood that it was possible that other people might overreact in fear if they saw the Candonite children, perhaps take them to jail or worse, to a laboratory in some creepy secret underground hideout.

"My mom is really great," Peter said, trying to ease his friends' fears as he climbed out of the boat. He looked around to make sure the coast was clear and gestured for Angela and Joe to follow.

Inside they found Peter's mother in the kitchen making Peter a snack. She was pouring milk into a glass and turned when she heard Peter. She had cookies on a plate in her other hand. Peter tossed the mail on the counter, took the cookies from his mom, and swiftly threw them into a drawer. He knew it wouldn't be good if Joe and Angela saw him eating them.

"If you don't want cookies, Peter, just say so! I could have saved those for your dad!" she said, setting the glass of milk on the counter.

"Mom, it's not that. I have guests," he said.

"I could always make more," she said, turning toward the pantry door. "Who are your guests? Is Lina here early?"

"No mom, it isn't Lina. And *please* don't make any more cookies!" Peter said.

Peter's mom turned from the pantry door to face Peter. Then she saw the Candonite children walk into the room. She took a step back and gasped.

Peter smiled softly. "Mom, I would like you to meet my new friends, Joe and Angela."

Peter's mom said nothing. She didn't even blink.

"Mom!" Peter said. "Mom!" He repeated, a little louder.

She spoke abruptly and startled the children. "Yes?"

"Are you all right?" Peter asked.

"I will be in a moment," his mother said as her face softened and her body relaxed. "Excuse me. Where are my manners? Nice to meet you!" she said, walking over to the Candonites. "Peter told me you were real, but I didn't believe him." She examined them in amazement.

"Nice to meet you, Mrs. Fischer," Angela and Joe said.

"This is amazing! Peter, I am sorry I didn't believe you," his mom said, pulling him close to her side for a squeeze. "I will never doubt you again."

"It's okay, Mom." Peter squeezed her back.

"Well, I know Peter is hungry. Would you two like a snack? I could make ham and cheese crackers," Peter's mom said.

"Yes, thank you," Angela and Joe replied. They were very hungry. They hadn't eaten since the garden.

"Would you mind if we took a few moments to clean up?" Angela asked.

"Oh my, you do need some cleaning up, don't you?" Peter's mother said as she led them to the bathroom.

Peter poured the milk and his mother made the snack. Peter wasn't surprised at how easygoing his mom was being. She always handled everything with ease. His father often told the story of when she was in labor with Peter. Instead of going to the hospital right away to give birth, she did her hair and makeup, washed a load of laundry, and cooked dinner. He said he practically picked her up and took her to the hospital where Peter was born two hours later.

Peter's mother went around the house nonchalantly closing all the blinds. When she returned, they all sat at the kitchen table eating and talking. The Candonite children expressed how they were afraid because they didn't know how to get home. Even worse, they didn't know how other humans might react. Mrs. Fischer told Angela and Joe not to worry. When her husband got home, they would figure out how to get them back to Maple Town.

"Your dad will be home in an hour, Peter. I should call him and give him a heads-up," his mom said, moving toward the phone.

"Hi honey," she said when she reached Peter's father. "I wanted to let you know we will be having a couple more guests for dinner tonight. Peter's Candonite friends, Angela and Joe....No, this isn't a joke! I am serious! I haven't lost my mind....I love you, see you soon."

"Does Dad believe you, Mom?" Peter asked anxiously.

"He will when he sees Joe and Angela. I better get dinner started." She winked.

Breaking the News

Peter, Angela, and Joe were in the kitchen helping Peter's mom when Peter's dad came home. He hung up his blazer, placed his keys in the drawer by the front door, and let out a big sigh like he always did when he came home at the end of a workday. Peter's body tensed and a sense of nervous excitement rushed over him. *What will Dad do?* They could hear Mr. Fischer's footsteps on the wooden floor as he headed toward the kitchen.

Peter's dad started talking before he even entered the room. "Now, what is all this nonsense?" As he entered the kitchen, his expression was almost identical to what Peter's mother's looked like earlier when she had come face-to-face with the Candonite children.

It took Peter's dad a bit longer to comprehend that Candonite children were actually standing in his kitchen than it had for Peter's mother. Peter's dad had to sit and put his head down on the table between his hands, peeking up over his glasses every once in a while. He even took off his glasses once and wiped them clean just in case he might be seeing things. He obviously wasn't.

Peter's mom gave his dad a glass of water and

told the children, "Kids, give me a few moments with my husband before Lina gets here for dinner."

The children did as they were told. Peter couldn't wait until his friend got there. He had tried calling her earlier, but there was no answer. He knew she would love to hear the news. Lina had been with Peter in Maple Town during his adventures. Now there was proof for others to see that their story was real and not the product of overactive imaginations.

After some time, Peter's mother called for him to set the table. *Everything must be fine*, he thought. Joe and Angela sat side-by-side across from Peter. Peter's mother and his father sat across from one another. Every once in a while Peter's dad would say something like, "This is weird. I must be dreaming. You do smell very nice."

There was a knock at the door. Peter ran to open it. Lina and her little brother Henry stood in the doorway. Lina once said that Henry was the sort of little brother you wanted to sell in a yard sale for twenty-five cents and at the end of the day, if no one bought him, mark him down and put him in the free box next to the orphaned socks and the holey underwear.

"Peter, your mom said it was all right if I brought Henry over whenever I wanted. Well, I didn't want to, but he kept begging." She handed him a plastic container. "Here, my mom made lumpia. You better take it before Henry eats it all."

"Lumpia?"

"Yes, sorta like Filipino egg rolls," Lina said.

"I want to hear more about the Candy people," Henry blurted out.

Lina shrugged. "Henry is the only one who believes me about our adventure."

Peter couldn't contain himself. He tugged at Lina. "They are here!"

"Who?"

"Angela and Joe!" Peter answered, excited.

"Quit joking, Peter. I am hungry. I am not in the mood for jokes," Lina said.

"I'm not joking. Really, they are here, in the kitchen. Come on!" he said as he closed the door behind them and shoved them toward the kitchen.

Lina wasn't sure what to think. Two days ago, if someone had told her that Candonite people were in Peter's kitchen, she would have thought they were loony. After being to Maple Town, nothing seemed impossible now. She sniffed the air and a smile illuminated her face.

Once all of them were inside the kitchen, Peter thought Henry was never going to stop jabbering at the Candonites. "Can I touch you? Do you come in different flavors? How can you live without eating sweets?"

Everyone had come to the conclusion that they should keep the Candonites' being in town hush-hush. No need to stir up anyone. No need to cause any alarm to people who might not understand. Of course, Peter and Lina knew this might be a bit hard for Henry. Lina made him promise not to tell anyone about Angela and Joe, at least until the Candonite children were safely home, or else she wouldn't tell him stories about her trip to Maple Town anymore.

After dinner, to give Joe and Angela a minute of peace from her nagging little brother, Lina told Henry to go and watch some TV. He was reluctant at first, but Lina told him she was sure a cartoon movie he wanted to watch was on. Henry got up from his chair and went to the family room.

A little while later, Henry shouted, "This TV is broken. The same thing is on every channel!"

"I better go help him before he comes back in here and bugs you guys again," Lina said, heading to the family room. Peter followed to see what Henry was talking about.

Peter and Lina couldn't believe what they were seeing on the TV. At the bottom of the screen in flashing red letters outlined in white were the words "BREAKING NEWS!" A newscaster was yelling into his microphone that it was the first time in his career he had seen anything like this. He seemed very nervous, looking over his shoulder constantly.

He continued, "No one has been hurt. Earlier today, eyewitnesses stated seeing massively large beings that appeared to be made of pebbles or rocks. They seemed to have appeared out of nowhere. Witnesses report seeing some kind of box. If I heard correctly, the pebbled people shot out of the box and landed at the intersection of Harrison and Bernard Street, leaving a giant crater in the road. No one seems to know why they are here or what they want. Where they are at the present time is not clear. In a moment, I am going to talk to eyewitnesses who got a closer look."

The camera panned to a young couple holding hands tightly and an older gentleman dressed in a suit and tie. They looked extremely anxious. "One eyewitness, Horace Bloomfield, said he witnessed the pebbled people apprehend police officers at the Community Police Officer of the Year Awards ceremony," said the newscaster, nearly sticking his microphone up Horace's nose. "Tell our viewers all about it, Horace."

Horace began, "I believe every cop in town has been detained by those horrible creatures. The pebbled people are very strong and I saw one break down a door with a single blow. They're big, really big. Bigger than any human being I have encountered. I'd say the shortest were probably seven feet. The one who seemed to be in command was easily nine feet." The cameraman left Horace's face and panned over his shoulder quickly. The lens was moving too fast to see anything, but they could hear shrieks. Then the cameraman panned back to where Horace was giving his interview.

Peter's and Lina's hearts skipped a beat as they stared at Goaltan himself, who was now holding the microphone. Those were dark eyes they never had wanted to look into again.

"I don't want to watch this. I want to watch my cartoon," Henry whined.

"Be quiet, Henry. Not now!" Lina scolded.

By now the others had come into the family room. Everyone gasped. Henry turned his attention to Peter's comic books on the coffee table and quickly tuned out everything else.

Peter and everyone else came to the conclusion that Goaltan and the Peblars had somehow come to their town. *But how?*

Suddenly the cameraman dropped the camera and said, "I don't get paid enough for this. I am out of here!"

Long pebbled fingers came across the screen. The camera was turned upright and fixed back on Goaltan, the fingers moving away from the screen.

Goaltan spoke. "Boy, I know you are out there somewhere and I know you have something to do with my standing here right now. Part of me wants to thank you for freeing me from my foul lair, the other part of me wants to pulverize you. Since I am not much of the thanking type, I choose to find you and make you pay for saving your two little Candonite friends and bringing me here to this world. Here is the deal: I will destroy every pie, every cupcake, every lollipop, and everything else you consider a sweet treat until none exist! I will destroy every store, every restaurant, every coffee shop, every bakery, every place that carries even a morsel of what you consider tasty delicacies until you show me your face. Don't even think about leaving town. I have that covered. All three exits out of town are blocked. There is no way in or out. I will start in the morning at 7:00 a.m. sharp. Every hour on the hour after that—well, you will see!" Goaltan paused to let out a ferocious roar. "Meet me right here. Oh, and bring the human girl!"

The television went black.

Everyone in the room let out another gasp.

Peter looked at the others and said with concern, "What about Papa's Sweet Shop?"

Peter's father put his finger over his lips and motioned to everyone except Henry to move back into the kitchen. No need to disturb Henry.

I Knew It!

It was 5:00 a.m. Henry and Lina had long since gone home. Peter remembered watching the clock until almost 1:00 a.m. He could hear the faint clinking of glasses downstairs and recognized the smell of brewed coffee. Peter suspected that no one had slept very well. He recalled the night before, with everyone in the neighborhood scrambling to clear their homes of anything belonging in the sweets category. He looked out the window a few times, watching the neighbors scamper to the curb with their trash cans. A couple of them had talked nervously with each other as they stuffed cookies and donuts into the trash. Occasionally, some of the treats made it to their mouths in a desperate effort to get rid of anything that would give Goaltan a reason to strike. Peter couldn't imagine a world without sugary confections. He didn't want to imagine never being able to come home to fresh-baked cookies again.

He whispered toward the floor, where the Candonite children were curled up in sleeping bags. "You guys asleep?"

"No," Angela replied.

"Been awake a half hour," Joe answered.

Peter sat up in bed, still whispering. "Do you think Lina's mom and dad will let her go to Goaltan?"

"No way! Lina's mother was very upset when she came to pick her up last night and her dad said he was going to lock her in her room. Henry enthusiastically volunteered to keep watch," said Angela.

"Papa's Sweet Shop! I have to keep it safe. It will be my fault if it gets destroyed," Peter said, ashamed.

"What are we going to do? I keep asking myself the same question over and over," Joe said.

"Me too," Angela replied.

"I know what *I* am going to do," Peter said, lowering himself to the floor. "I have to find a way to get to Lina. Her parents took her home before I had a chance to talk to her alone."

"Peter, what makes you think your parents are going to let you go? They didn't like that idea either," Angela reminded him.

Peter reflected on the night before. The phone should have rung several times. Papa and Nana would have called if they had seen the news. Lina would have wanted to talk to him for sure. He suspected it was like that all around town. Goaltan and his friends had found a way to stop them from using the phone lines. When Peter's father had picked up the phone to call Papa, the line was dead. It sent a chill down his spine. *There has to be a way*, Peter thought.

Since the three of them couldn't sleep, they

headed downstairs. Peter's parents sat at the table. "Hello," they said with forced smiles. There was no "Good morning" greeting since it was not a very good one. His father quickly got up to whip up some eggs and toast. Peter's dad made breakfast nearly every morning, unless he had an early appointment. On those mornings, Peter and his mother would have cereal and orange juice. Peter was surprised his father felt in the mood to make anything this morning. He looked around the table and everyone looked so tired. No one said anything. Instead they set the table and when that was done, fidgeted with placemats and napkins.

When the food was on the table and after his first bite, Peter asked anxiously, "Dad, what are we going to do? We can't just let Goaltan destroy Papa's Sweet Shop and all the other places in town he talked about."

"I don't know son, I don't know," his dad answered, not looking up from his coffee cup. It seemed strange for him to be drinking coffee out of a smiley-face mug that read, "Have a great day!"

Breakfast was very glum. No one said much. Everyone was too busy trying to figure out what to do and watching the clock closely. It was already 5:49 a.m., a little over an hour until Goaltan would start smashing things up.

Peter watched the minutes turn on the clock. Suddenly there was a knock at the door that scared everyone. Joe knocked over his milk and Peter's mom quickly wiped it up. *Who could it be? Lina? The police? Goaltan?* Peter looked at his dad for advice about what to do next. Peter's dad paused for a moment and then got up from the table and headed to the door. Peter's mom put down the rag she was holding and grabbed her husband's hand as he walked past. She squeezed it and he returned the squeeze and smiled a half smile. Everyone held their breath as the door opened. They listened carefully.

"What a relief! Mom and Pops, you're here!" Peter's dad called out louder than normal for everyone to hear. *All right! Nana & Papa!* Peter immediately felt a little safer knowing they were there. Papa always knew what to do in any situation.

Peter had not yet had a chance to talk to his grandparents. Papa had just dropped him off at home after he returned from Maple Town. No one then had believed him about his adventure, though Peter was almost certain Nana had been to Maple Town in her youth. At that moment, he wanted nothing more than to find out.

Peter ran into the living room and threw his arms around Nana. She was giggling when she embraced him, so happy to see him. Peter said, "Nana, I have been waiting forever to ask you a question." She smiled slyly as if she knew what the question would be. Peter continued, "Have you been to Maple Town? Have you seen the Candonites?"

Nana answered matter-of-factly, "No, I have never been to Maple Town." Disappointment spread across Peter's face. He was certain she had been there.

"I have been to Honeyville, though," she quickly added. "I believe it is the next town over. And yes, Peter, I have seen Candonites!"

"I knew it! I knew it! You did sign the guest book!" Peter felt like he had won a zillion bucks.

"At first, I didn't remember Honeyville," she continued. "Your Papa was telling me about how you told him that I had been to Maple Town and seen the Candonites. You see, Peter, that was so long ago and no one believed me. Everyone told me it was a dream, a very imaginative dream. Your great-grandmother even told me to never speak of it again, because she was afraid people would think oddly of me. I began to believe them. I never spoke of it again. Soon it did become a dream to me and regretfully, I forgot it entirely. It wasn't until I saw the news this morning that I remembered a smidgen of my adventures. And now I remember a little bit more." Nana smiled, warming Peter's heart.

"I am sorry I didn't believe you Peter. Please forgive this old man," Papa said, bending down to Peter's face.

"I forgive you, Papa."

"Thank you, Peter," Papa said, pushing his glasses back on the bridge of his nose.

Joe and Angela entered the room. Papa looked as though he would fall over as he slumped down onto the arm of a recliner in amazement. Nana had a very different reaction, jumping with delight and clapping her hands. Peter had never seen her jump before. He didn't think she could. Nana moved closer toward the children to take a better look. "You smell as I remembered! You look as I remembered! So simply wonderful, you are!" She kissed both of them on the forehead as if they were her own grand-children. Everyone in the room chuckled except for Papa, who was still staring with his mouth hanging wide open.

"Are you okay, Papa?" Peter asked.

It took Papa a moment to respond. His mouth formed into a half smile. "I will be. Papa needs a moment to let this all sink in."

Just then Peter's dad exclaimed, "The TV! You said the news was on." He scrambled for the remote.

"Yes, it came on earlier. Every channel has that dreadful Goaltan and his monstrous minions. What did he call them again?" Nana asked.

"Peblars," everyone answered in unison.

Peter's dad turned on the TV. Goaltan was once again taking up most of the TV screen, with a crowd of Peblars behind him. It was strange to see them standing in the intersection of Harrison and Bernard, a short driving distance from his house. Peter and his mother went to the local farmers' market almost every week, crossing through that intersection. *Now what roads were they supposed to take?* Peter thought. In addition to fruits and vege-tables, they would buy three delicious scones with warm boysenberry jam, one for each member of his family. He thought about the nice lady who ran the stand, Margaret. Every once in a while if they arrived late in the day, she would throw in an extra scone. If Goaltan got to her stand that would make Peter very upset.

Goaltan was talking now. "Human boy, I won't settle for just the girl. I want both of you."

Everyone in the room started looking around. What did he mean? He didn't know where Lina lived, did he? The camera panned wider. There at the end of Goaltan's wide reach was Lina, his brawny hand gripping her shoulder. She spoke softly straight into the camera. "Sorry, P. I only meant to case out the joint. I didn't mean to get caught." She looked so small and fragile in his clutch.

Goaltan mocked her. "Yes, she is soooooo sorry. She never meant to get caught. Silly girl!"

"You shut your veggie hole! You won't get away with this!" Lina tried to kick him, but his grip kept her from doing so.

Peter's mother gasped, followed by a series of worried replies from everyone around the room.

"Oh! No!"

"What was Lina thinking?"

"Poor Lina."

"What are we going to do?"

Goaltan brought their focus back to the screen. "By the way, Mr. P, that is what I will address you as from now on, since your little girlfriend won't tell me your name. How loyal. You have fifty-five minutes to show your face or I start destroying things around here!" The TV went black once more.

In other circumstances, Peter would have been embarrassed having Lina referred to as his girlfriend. However, there was no time for embarrassment. Peter didn't know exactly what they were going to do but he did know he was going to save his best friend. She would do the same for him. She was so brave to even go out there in the first place to check things out. Peter wondered if Lina's parents knew where she was. He pictured Lina's mother yelling at Goaltan through the television set.

Peter predicted it wouldn't be long until Goaltan found out who Peter was. All Goaltan had to do was scare some unsuspecting kid who went to school with Lina into telling him the identity of Mr. P. Lina would probably want to kick the kid for giving up the information, but it wouldn't matter. Goaltan would have what he wanted.

"We have to do something!" Peter shrilled.

"I know we do, Peter, but *what* is the question," Peter's dad said.

Peter knew it wasn't like they could ask Goaltan nicely to leave and let Lina go. There had to be a plan. And the plan had to be good and fast. Papa always had the answer, but one look at Papa and Peter could tell this time he didn't.

"I wish I could remember more, Peter, maybe then I could help," Nana said, looking like she was straining to remember. "The only thing new I have to report was that the little Candonite girl's house I stayed at was named Alyssa. She was a beautiful light blue rock-candy girl. She was so nice. I remember her telling me that she was a rare Candonite. There weren't many of her kind."

Peter quickly piped up. "Goaltan is of the rock-candy race. I mean he *was* of the rock-candy race. Goaltan looks and smells as he does now because he was so filled with hatred toward the townspeople for banishing him after years of causing havoc in the town. He was so unforgiving that his heart became solid rock and the rest of him slowly turned into pebbles. He became a rotted Candonite and turned into a Peblar."

"That is what the legend says and I believe it," Joe added.

"Me too," Angela agreed.

"Mom, try harder to remember and let us know if you remember anything of interest," Peter's mother said to Nana.

"I will, dear," Nana answered.

"All this is too much for Papa to comprehend, candy people standing right here in front of me. This is beyond amazing! This is a long way from my small humble hometown in Germany." Papa finally seemed a little more like himself. "Come. Sit down, all of you. We will sort this out." He told Joe and Angela to sit on either side of Nana, hoping that it would spark memories to help her remember her trip to

Honeyville.

"Not to rush, but we have only forty-nine minutes," Peter reminded everyone, looking at his watch.

Taking a deep breath and closing her eyes, Nana inhaled the sugary scents of the Candonite children. Everyone watched her, not daring to make a noise. For what seemed like forever she was silent. Her lips parted unexpectedly into a smile, the kind of smile you make when you haven't seen someone you love for a very long time. For another long minute she said nothing.

"I remember!" Nana exclaimed, her eyes still closed. No one said anything for fear she might lose those thoughts. "Oh my goodness, I ate too many goodies that night. I overdid it and I certainly shouldn't have. My mother had baked so many delightful things for the church bake sale, and said I could have two cookies before heading to bed. Well, I didn't think that was fair. Why did the bake sale get to have all those goodies when I could only have two cookies? I didn't care if my mother said eating too many sweets before bedtime would give me nightmares. I crept downstairs when my parents went outside to sit on the porch like they often do, my mother to read her book and my dad to search the skies with his telescope."

"Mom," Peter's dad said, in a tone that reminded her there wasn't much time for all the details.

Nana never opened her eyes while she continued. "When I was done with my delicious deceit, I was returning the kitchen to its rightful order when I opened the refrigerator. I could have sworn I never saw that little box in there before."

Peter knew what Nana was about to say next. Similar experiences with a special delivery box had just happened to Lina and him.

She continued, "Those red words 'Special Delivery' were glowing curiously as I opened the box, and within moments I found myself in a world so wonderfully magnificent! Oh, the gorgeous blue-green grass and those funny pointing trees!"

"Mom, do you remember anything that might help us?" Peter's dad pressed.

"Fast forward, dear," Papa encouraged her.

"I'll try," she answered, her eyes remaining shut. She seemed to be concentrating harder. She didn't speak for a couple minutes, then said, "I can't, I can't! I am watching it like a picture show." She opened her eyes in disappointment.

"It is all right, Mom," Peter's dad assured her. "You just keep watching and fill us in if you see anything useful." He peered down at his watch.

Nana seemed to like that idea. Peter didn't blame her. Thinking of Maple Town and Honeyville would be a gazillion times better than thinking about Goaltan and his grimy hands on Lina. Peter would have to wait to hear the whole glorious story. Everyone except Nana faced the table. It was now or never.

Not So Happy Donuts

Peter, his dad, and Papa climbed into the SUV. The others stayed behind. No need for everyone to go and they certainly didn't want Goaltan to find out that the Candonite children were in town. Originally, Peter was supposed to stay behind too. After he told his dad and Papa he had been to Goaltan's castle and joining them now couldn't be any more dangerous, they considered it. After he told them that Lina was his best friend and he wasn't going to take no for an answer, they agreed to let him go.

The three of them still were not sure what they were going to do, but they already had a place to start. Peter looked behind his seat and saw all the goodies they had collected from the neighborhood garbage cans. No one who saw them doing this seemed to mind, probably because they were eager to get rid of the sugary treats. Peter looked out the back window as he saw Lina's dad's car barreling down the road straight for the driveway.

"Wait, Dad!" Peter called out.

The car stopped within inches of the SUV. Lina's mother was scolding her husband in a foreign language as she exited the car. Peter could make out a few English words: "Kill us...Henry...car!" Peter knew she was upset by her husband's driving. She touched her forehead, moved down to touch her lower chest, and onto both shoulders and said, "Thank the good Lord!" She opened the back door and helped Henry, who wasn't moving fast enough for her, out of the car. Henry had on earphones and was playing a handheld video game. He didn't even look up. Lina's dad exited the car. Peter thought to himself that Lina's dad was one of those muscular guys you don't know are buff until they have a short sleeve shirt on. Peter remembered Lina telling him he used to be in the Navy, some kind of an officer. Peter had asked Lina if he had ever arrested anyone and Lina swatted him on the shoulder saying, "Not that kind of an officer, silly!"

Peter's dad told Peter and Papa, "Stay put. I will only be a minute."

Peter watched, leaning out the car window.

"We don't have much time. We have a plan we are hoping will work. It isn't much, but it is all we've got. We have to go now and we could use all the help we can get," Peter's dad said urgently.

"Take Henry inside," Lina's dad said to his wife, pushing his blond hair out of the way to wipe some sweat from his brow. "I am going with them."

"You bring me back Lina," she told her husband, grabbing his hand.

He bent down to kiss her on her forehead and mustered a small smile. "I will." He reached over and ruffled his son's hair. Henry didn't even flinch. He was too busy playing his game.

Inside the car, Lina's dad introduced himself as Rod. Peter's dad explained the plan to Rod as they drove closer to their destination.

No other cars were on the roads. Everyone was too busy staying out of sight. Everyone except for old man Rupert, who was in his garden, as he usually was, fiddling around with a stick of black licorice dangling out of his mouth. He looked up as they drove by. They didn't have time to stop and tell him he better get rid of the licorice. Perhaps old man Rupert knew about Goaltan and didn't care. He was best known by all the kids at school for being a frightening grouchy old man. Peter looked into some of the local business buildings and didn't see anyone. It was so odd to see his normally bustling town so quiet. It gave him chills.

They stopped at a dumpster in an alley to get more discarded treats. They also stopped at Nana's and Papa's house, which was on the way. They were going to be cutting it close to the 7:00 a.m. deadline. Peter wasn't sure why they were stopping at his grandparents' house, just that Papa was adamant that they did. Papa told everyone to wait in the car and he would be back soon. The next thing Peter knew, the garage door was opening and Papa was holding three objects in his hand. As Papa moved closer to the car, he realized they were helmets: one jet black with brilliant red flames, one cherry red with fluorescent pink flowers, and the third royal blue. It was then that Peter noticed the mopeds behind Papa.

Everyone got out of the car and Peter's dad said, "Whoa, Dad! What? You have mopeds?"

Peter stood there wide-eyed with his mouth hanging open. *Papa and Nana on mopeds! No way!*

Papa slyly grinned. "Yes son, your mother and I have been riding for the last six months."

"This is crazy. Why didn't you tell me?" Peter's dad asked.

"Because you would say it was crazy," Papa answered matter-of-factly.

"What are we going to do with those?" Peter's dad questioned.

"Son, we are going to need a quick getaway. We can't very well run out of there on foot all the way home. I am fit, but I am not as spry as I used to be. I would surely get caught."

"Why do you have three helmets?" Peter's dad asked.

"In case I got around to telling you and you let Peter go along on a ride." Papa grinned, winking at Peter.

"I don't know about this," Peter's dad said, pursing his lips.

"I assure you, I am a very safe driver, much better than in the car. Your mom and I took several safety classes and we are members of the Rockin' Peds Elite," Papa said proudly.

Peter's dad wasn't quite sure how to respond.

He didn't like the idea one bit, but agreed it was better to have multiple getaway vehicles. Papa and Rod mounted the mopeds and rolled them out of the driveway. As Peter strapped on his helmet, he saw it had golden lightning bolts on the sides. Peter liked that immensely. He hopped on Papa's jet-black moped and was impressed to see that it had red and yellow flames. He glanced over at Nana's moped and had to smile when he saw Rod, all muscle, wearing a flowery helmet. When Rod pulled ahead on Nana's cherry-red moped, Peter let out a chuckle at the sight of the skull with a pink bow in its hair painted on the back of the moped. *All right, Nana!*

Peter's dad led the mopeds in his SUV. As they got closer to Harrison and Bernard Streets the air became icy cold. The hair on Peter's arms was standing up and goose bumps started to form on his skin.

"What is that smell?" Papa yelled, squishing up his nose. Peter knew exactly what that rancid smell was: the Peblars. The smell was worse than burning rotten broccoli and onions. It wouldn't be long before the entire town felt icy cold and smelled like a smoldering sewer.

When they thought they couldn't go any further without being detected, Peter's dad pulled the SUV down an alleyway and the others followed on their mopeds. They were going in blindly. They had no idea how many Peblars there were or in which areas the brutes would be hanging out.

"We have to time this exactly right or we will

be in a heap of trouble," Peter's dad said, swallowing hard. In an effort to lighten the mood, in his best secret agent voice he added, "All right men, our mission is to save Lina and we'll worry about how to get rid of Goaltan and his goons later." It didn't lighten the mood.

Papa took his son's face in his hands, looked straight into his eyes and said, "Be careful, Son. I love you."

"You be careful, too, Dad. I love you," Mr. Fischer replied.

"I love you both," Peter said. He grabbed his father around the waist and squeezed as hard as he could. He squeezed so hard his arms hurt. Then he did the same to Papa.

"Let's get my little girl back!" Rod said confidently and fist-bumped with everyone. Peter's dad looked a little awkward during the motion.

Peter took off his helmet and handed it to Rod, then climbed into the back seat of the SUV as the others drove down the opposite street. It was 6:56 a.m.

The plan was simple enough. Peter's dad was to drive the SUV down Harrison Street, open the trunk with the release on his car keys, and swing a hard left. Hopefully the confections they had collected would go flying along the road and distract Goaltan and the Peblars. Meanwhile, Papa and Rod were to drive up Bernard and hopefully spot Lina quickly enough to get her on the back of Nana's moped.

It would be dangerous. Peter had firsthand experience with what Goaltan was capable of doing. Just days before, Peter had witnessed Goaltan's abilities when he and Lina rescued Joe and Angela from Goaltan's lair. Now he was attempting to rescue Lina. He took a deep breath and braced for the ride.

As they drove closer to the corner of Harrison and Bernard, the buildings began to look as though Goaltan was making his home away from home. They were covered with tiny gray pebbles, just like the ones that made up Goaltan's castle.

"Whoa!" Peter's dad said.

Peter rolled down the window in preparation and felt the frosty air pour into the vehicle. The smell was putrid, reminding him once again of Goaltan's dreadful home. What he saw next he couldn't believe, or didn't want to believe. Where Happy Donuts once stood was now a gaping hole. The ground was covered with rubble. Happy Donuts really was a happy place. Peter went there every first Sunday of the month before church with his Nana and Papa.

Happy was a really cool guy. He always called Peter "little dude" and gave him a free donut hole while they waited for their order. Nana was always saying that Happy was quite the gentlemen. Peter glanced at his watch. It wasn't 7:00 a.m. yet. Goaltan hadn't kept his promise. He wasn't supposed to start destroying anything unless Peter didn't show up for Lina. Peter could feel his face burning with anger.

Happy didn't deserve this.

"Hang on, son, here we go!" Peter's dad exclaimed as he pressed hard on the gas pedal.

Peter looked straight forward and could see several Peblars turning their heads toward them as the engine roared louder. He searched for Goaltan and Lina. No sign of either one.

Peter had a surge of energy and leaned out the window to scream as loud as he could, "I am here now, you big oaf—7:00 o'clock on the dot!" He reached in the back and threw a cherry pie in the Peblars' direction. As soon as the words exited his mouth, he saw Goaltan head for the middle of the street straight ahead of him, holding Lina by her shoulder with his burly hand. She was trying to kick and bite him with no luck.

"Oh spam!" Peter shouted as they barreled straight toward them. This was a term Peter used when he wanted to say something he wasn't supposed to. His mother didn't seem to mind it and had even said it a few times herself.

Peter's dad turned the steering wheel sharply to the left. Even though Peter expected it, the sudden move still surprised him. Goaltan's eyes enlarged with rage as he saw what happened next. The tasty morsels flew straight out of the back of the vehicle. Peter helped by throwing what he could out the window. Goaltan released his grip on Lina. She ran toward her dad and Papa, two blurs on the road. Peter wasn't so sure about Papa's driving, but he seemed to be maneuvering the moped with precision. Peblars were clawing at them as the mopeds whistled by toward Lina. One Peblar narrowly missed Papa. Goaltan wasn't paying attention to Lina, which was a good thing. The bad thing, he was paying attention to Peter.

Peter's dad drove the SUV up over the curb and struggled to get back on the street. Peter tried hard to keep his eyes on Goaltan and Lina. He breathed a sigh of relief as Lina mounted the moped with her father. Peter couldn't hear what Goaltan was yelling, but was pretty sure it was something his mother wouldn't want him to hear. Goaltan raised his right arm above his head and Peter understood this was not good.

Peter looked over his shoulder and saw a crack in the road moving toward them, faster and faster, and growing bigger and bigger with every foot.

"Dad, you better step on it!" Peter cried.

Peter's dad pushed his foot down hard on the gas pedal.

"Dad!" Peter yelled.

His father could see what was going on in the rearview mirror. Peter didn't know what his dad was going to do next, but he better do something now.

The crackling grew louder—almost to a thunder—when they felt the back of the SUV being lifted two to three feet off the ground. As fast as it was lifted, the SUV dropped back to the ground and continued to move steadily ahead. The thundering had stopped and Peter looked out the back window to see a crater the width of the street behind them. Goaltan had missed. In the distance, he could see Goaltan jumping up and down in frustration, causing the street to ripple. They were safe for now.

Unexpected Visitor

Pulling into their garage, Peter and his dad let out gigantic sighs of relief. They were home, but where was the rest of the rescue team? He hoped they weren't far behind. Peter thought it was a little peculiar that some of the neighbors were peeping out their windows at them. He thought maybe it was because no one else dared to drive around. Seconds later, Papa arrived, waving triumphantly. Peter and his dad waited for him before they went inside where they were met by hugs and kisses.

"That was the most action I have seen in years!" Papa said.

"Is my Lina with you?" Mrs. Young asked desperately.

"They should be right behind us," Papa assured her.

Mrs. Young rushed to the window to wait and Peter joined her.

"We got separated shortly after Lina jumped on the moped with her dad. A crazed Peblar jumped in front of our mopeds and nearly swiped my head off! I was rattled but I managed to continue straight down the road. Rod swerved and took a right turn to avoid a collision," Papa said.

"Oh!" Mrs. Young gasped.

"Don't worry. I am sure they will be here any moment," Papa reassured everyone.

"We saw you on TV. You were all so brave!" Nana said.

"You did?" Papa answered, looking at the black TV screen.

"Oh yes, dear! My goodness! All of you looked like superheroes rushing in to save the day!" Nana added.

Peter's mother explained, "Goaltan appeared on TV a few minutes before 7:00 a.m. talking about how he wanted everyone to watch as he made Lina and Peter his personal slaves. Goaltan said since he doesn't plan on returning to his own land, he was going to make Peter and Lina pay for what the Candonites did to him so many years ago, when they banished him from Maple Town and Honeyville. Well, when you showed up things didn't go as Goaltan had planned and he was livid. The camera shut off soon after that."

"You showed him!" Angela said with spunk, her rainbow chips swaying.

"I would have felt awful if you were captured this time by Goaltan right after rescuing us," Joe said.

"It is an awful shame about Happy Donuts," Nana added.

"Quite a shame," Papa agreed.

Peter looked around and didn't see Henry.

"Where is Henry?" he asked.

"I hope you don't mind, Peter. I let him play with the action figures in your room. Something to keep him busy, honey," Peter's mother answered. Normally he would have minded. However, Peter understood the situation. Hopefully Henry wouldn't pull off any of the heads. He tried not to think about it.

"They're here!" Mrs. Young shouted, heading for the door.

Elated, Peter watched as the moped drove into the garage. Lina was ecstatically waving at him. He raced to the door to greet them.

Once inside, Lina told about how she had snuck out in the early morning hours. Lina apologized to her parents and added that she knew they would never have let her go. She had to do it.

"Dad, you are always telling me about your duties you had in the military. Well, I had my own duties to fulfill," she told him. To Peter's surprise, Rod shook his head like he understood. Lina continued, "When I thought I was within range of the Peblars, I climbed a tall tree." Mrs. Young didn't like the sound of that and let out a disapproving noise that came from smacking her tongue against the roof of her mouth.

"Ah, Mom, you know I am an excellent climber! You always say I get my climbing skills from my lola, Grandma is still a great climber," Lina said lightly. "Anyway, I picked a good tree. I could see

Goaltan and his thugs clearly. I also heard a low crackling noise and saw the side of a nearby house very slowly turning into small gray pebbles until the whole house looked like something straight out of Goaltan's homeland. That was bizarre! I watched for a few minutes, scoping out the area. When I thought I got enough info, I climbed back down the tree and was about to sprint out of there. The next thing I knew, a Peblar had me by my arm and was pulling me toward their camp. I fought as hard as I could, Dad. But he was just too strong." Lina looked disappointed in herself.

Rod put his hands on Lina's shoulders and said, "You are safe now, soldier." At that moment, Peter recognized where Lina got her tough-girl spirit.

Lina continued, "Goaltan likes to hear himself talk as much as he likes scaring people. I promise I was getting the biggest headache listening to him ramble on. He told me about what happened after Peter and I rescued Joe and Angela. The special delivery box fell from thin air right onto his head. Goaltan said the next thing he knew he was being sucked into it. Many Peblars came to his aid, but the force of the box was too much. All of them ended up here at the corner of Harrison and Bernard within a matter of moments."

"Why did they emerge at that particular spot?" Angela asked.

"It is the center of town," Papa said.

"I think it has something to do with my messing up the natural order of things," Joe said, swallowing hard. "When Peter and Angela were touching the special delivery package and saying the words that would return them home, I had the not-so-brilliant idea of patting Peter on the back. Angela tried to stop me, but it was too late. We were sucked in too."

"It's all right, Joe. You didn't know," Peter said, trying to make his friend feel better.

"Nana, did you remember anything useful?" Peter's father asked.

"No. Sorry, Dear." She shut her eyes to get back to remembering.

"Well, I think we better not stay here too long. It isn't safe," Papa said.

"Where are we going to go?" Lina asked.

"We can't very well stay here. It will only be a matter of time before Goaltan finds out where we live," Papa said.

"I would like to say we could go to Papa's and Nana's house or the Sweet Shop, but neither would be a good idea," Peter concluded.

"We better figure out something fast," Peter's mother advised.

There was a knock at the door and everyone froze.

"I'll get it," Lina said. "If it is Goaltan he would have knocked the door down." Everyone relaxed, knowing she was right.

As the door opened, everyone heard, "Howdy!"

"Old man Rupert?" Lina blurted out. "I mean, Mr. Rupert, what are you doing here?"

"May I come in?" the old man asked. He spoke with a country accent and wore a stiff straw hat and grass-stained blue jean overalls.

"Of course, come in." Peter's mother waved him in and Lina stepped inside with her mouth agape.

Peter had never been this close to old man Rupert. He instinctively took a step back. No one had as much as spoken to the grumpy man, though they were yelled at occasionally when they walked too close to his fence or lingered on the sidewalk outside his home longer than a minute. Pretty much everyone stayed clear of his house whenever possible. It was kind of hard sometimes, since he lived a few houses down the street from Peter.

"Holy millennium!" Mr. Rupert exclaimed at the sight of Angela and Joe. He was so intrigued by them that he couldn't contain himself. He walked up to them and started sniffing and poking.

"Hey, watch it!" Angela said.

"Sorry. I would have never thought in all the years I have been alive, I would ever see the likes of y'all and your friend Goaltan," Mr. Rupert said.

"He is NOT our friend!" Joe said, offended.

"Oh, I humbly apologize," Mr. Rupert said. "Best be statin' my business."

"Yes, you best be," Angela agreed.

"I'm here 'cause I was watchin' y'all on the

tellervision. I figured everyone else in town probably was too. It wouldn't be long before ol' Goaltan himself figures out where y'all reside. I don't want no bully coming here and whoopin' up my neighborhood. I reckoned if y'all come to stay with me, ya'd be in a better position. Now, my place ain't nothin' fancy like this here home. But it is plenty big and would keep y'all safe," Mr. Rupert said.

Peter wasn't so sure it would be safer going to stay with Mr. Rupert than staying home. What he did know were the stories from the kids around the neighborhood. They were not pleasant stories.

Mr. Rupert must have been reading his mind. He said, "Now, I know what ya youngsters have been hearin' around town, but I ain't got nothin' strange or out of the ordinary in my home 'cept for my coin collection. I do keep to myself mostly, but that ain't no cause for alarm."

"What about when you yell at kids for leaning on your fence or lingering outside your house?" Lina asked.

"I was simply bein' cordial. They never stayed long enough to hear my invitation for freshly squeezed lemonade or a gingersnap cookie. I make the best of both! Don't know what got those nasty rumors started about me bein' a mean old fogy. It stings like a hornet at times. I can't see long distance worth a lick, so I recollect sometimes people might think I am mighty rude if I don't get to wavin' speedy quick," Mr. Rupert said, taking off his straw hat and revealing his tuft of gray hair. He waited politely for the answer, tapping the hat against his leg.

Peter was ashamed that he believed the kids at school before coming to his own conclusion. He told himself he would make a conscious effort to never do that again.

Papa spoke first. "I think that is a great idea. The only problem is how do we get to your house undetected? We don't want anyone to know we are there."

Mr. Rupert winked and gave a crooked smile. "I already thought that through."

He told everyone to hurry up and gather anything they thought they would want to take with them to his house. Mrs. Young fetched Henry, who was still upstairs playing with Peter's action figures. Thankfully, the heads were still attached. Henry had one in his hand when he came downstairs. Lina looked at Peter for approval and then grabbed a stack of Peter's comic books for Henry. She was pretty sure Mr. Rupert didn't have anything that Henry could play with and it was best to keep him occupied. Peter's mother and Angela went to the kitchen and grabbed supplies to make sandwiches for lunch and a casserole for dinner. No one knew how long they would have to stay at Mr. Rupert's. Rod took Joe and Peter's dad to the garage to get some provisions. Peter wasn't sure what kind of provisions they would be getting, but Rod seemed to know what was necessary for the situation. It probably had something to do with his military training. Peter felt like he should be gathering something too, but he had no idea what.

So he asked Mr. Rupert, "Is there anything you think I should bring?"

Mr. Rupert answered, "Well, I don't know how long y'all be stayin', but ya may want to grab some blankets in case ya have to stay the night."

Peter headed upstairs to get blankets when the TV came back on, with the pebbled fingers of the cameraman trying to focus on Goaltan. It was time to go. The idea was simple. Goaltan seemed to like being on TV and as Lina already said, he liked hearing himself talk. So it was only a matter of time until Goaltan made another appearance on TV. When he did, everyone in town would be glued to their television screens wondering what he had to say. The coast would be clear for them to make their way to Mr. Rupert's house where he had already planned ahead and set up a video recorder to record his TV. They would be able to watch what Goaltan had to say once they made it safely to the house.

F-I-S-H-E-R

When Peter and the others reached Mr. Rupert's house, they caught the tail end of Goaltan's speech. The words rang in their ears, "Peter and Lina, I am coming for you!"

Everyone stopped in the middle of whatever they were doing. Everyone, that is, except for Henry who was too busy checking out Mr. Rupert's things. He was looking into a china cabinet full of angel sculptures.

Mr. Rupert fidgeted with the video recorder and said, "Almost got this thing ready to roll. Make yourselves at home." Peter knew he was just trying to be polite, but "make yourselves at home" seemed a strange choice of words for that moment. No one could really relax enough to feel that comfortable now.

The video began playing. For a minute nothing happened. When Peter was about to suggest that Mr. Rupert fast forward, there was Goaltan in a close-up. The yellows of Goaltan's eyes where the whites of his eyes should be were a bright contrast to his deep, dark, almost black irises. The hair on the back of Peter's neck stood up.

Goaltan spoke. "As you can imagine, I am not

pleased! In fact, I am infuriated! You will not be making a fool out of me any further, Mr. P. I have someone here. I believe you know him." The camera panned out and there was an African-American boy with a baseball cap pulled down low over his eyes. He wasn't looking at the camera. Goaltan turned the boy's head toward the camera and flicked the baseball cap off his head in one smooth motion.

"Curtis Wheeler!" Lina and Peter exclaimed. Curtis was a kid from their school.

"Sorry, Peter and Lina. He made me tell or he was going to obliterate my mom's Cupcakery," Curtis said.

"Oh, my young friend, about that. I still plan on obliterating it!" Goaltan chuckled deeply.

"But you said if I told you who Peter and Lina were, you—"

"Enough of the whining, boy!" Goaltan shouted. A short stocky Peblar took Curtis by the arm and led him out of camera range.

The cameraman zoomed in for another close-up of Goaltan, who seemed very pleased with himself. "Peter Fischer and Lina Young, you have slipped out of my hands for the last time. No one makes a fool out of me, no one!" The cameraman panned to show the location of Goaltan and his Peblars. They were now outside of Curtis Wheeler's mother's shop, the Cupcakery. Goaltan, wearing a malicious grin, reached his hand offscreen and returned with an elegant-looking cupcake. Goaltan closed his massive pebbled hand, smashing the cupcake to smithereens. He laughed an evil laugh that lingered in the air and added, "Peter and Lina, I am coming for you!"

Peter and Lina simultaneously gulped.

Lina stood straight up and said, "He makes me so mad. What gives him the right?"

Everyone agreed.

Nana said, "I better get my eyes shut and get back to Honeyville, partly because it will make me more tranquil and partly because I have this nagging feeling it will help."

"Good idea, dear. Perhaps you can share with us out loud so we can all calm our nerves," Papa said.

Nana looked around the room. Everyone seemed to like the idea.

"I will keep watch," Rod said, moving toward the front window.

"I'll help," Mr. Rupert said, positioning himself by a narrow window next to the front door.

"We will rotate keeping watch. We don't know if Goaltan knows where we live or how long it will take him to find out," Peter's dad said.

"Curtis has never been to either of our houses so he couldn't have told Goaltan our addresses," Peter said.

"Hopefully if he looks in the phone book, he will spell Fischer wrong. F-I-S-H-E-R is a common misspelling of our last name," Peter's dad said.

"We aren't listed in the phone book. I don't

like all the solicitations," Rod said. Both statements gave everyone some relief.

Nana picked up where she left off. She instantly brought them to a much more pleasant state. Henry's mother told him to stop flicking Mr. Rupert's mini-cactus plant and sit on the couch to listen to Nana's story.

Saving the Best for Last

Nana was at the Honeyville Mall with her new Candonite friend, Alyssa. They had already been there for an hour and didn't have too much longer before Alyssa's mother was going to pick them up in their limousine hover car. Nana explained that Alyssa was from a very wealthy Candonite family. Alyssa's mother and father were inventors. There was a history of inventors in her family, every generation having successful inventors on both sides. Alyssa's mother and father were the most well-to-do because they were two geniuses who married one another. Alyssa was extremely disappointed because she believed she didn't inherit the inventing gene.

"It was as though the mall stores knew what a customer would be interested in purchasing," Nana said, reminiscing. "I walked up to a pet store display window and saw the cutest little white chocolate bunnies hopping around. The other display window was empty. After I admired the little animals for a few seconds, mechanical hands appeared. They pointed at me and moved up and down the length of my body from the other side of the glass. When they were done, they held up a finger as if to say, 'wait here.' The mechanical hands disappeared into the pet store and brought back something to the empty display window. It contained the perfect pets for me if I were going to be leaving with a pet that day. It was a tank full of lollipop tropical fish and gummy guppies. I just adore fish. I told the mechanical hands, 'Thank you, but I can't take the fish home.' Alyssa insisted there was another place we had to see before her mother picked us up, the toy store. Smack dab in the middle of the mall, Mr. Maxwell's Toy Store was a large cylinder-shaped store three stories high. No one ever went to the mall without at least peeking in the windows."

"I want to go there," Henry said, his mouth practically watering.

"I haven't even told you the best parts yet," Nana giggled, opening her eyes.

"Close those eyes back up. Let's not forget our original intentions for hearing your story," Mrs. Fischer reminded everyone. From then on no one interrupted, except to announce when they were switching lookouts for Goaltan and the Peblars.

Nana shut her eyes and returned to her story-telling. "It was unlike any toy store I had ever seen. The window constantly changed and displayed a different toy scene. Alyssa advised me to keep moving or the mechanical arm salesman would appear. Once inside, the first thing I noticed was that off to the left Candonite children were giggling as they got on pogo sticks and shot straight up to level two or three of the toy store, without using elevators or stairs. I heard laughter from the right side and saw three giant slides that intertwined around each other and stopped at each level of the store. Children were sliding down merrily to their floor destinations." Nana's body and hands helped the story along with movement as she told it.

"I was overwhelmed and had no idea where to begin, but thankfully Alyssa had a plan to see the best things. First, she had to introduce me to her uncle, Mr. Maxwell, the toy store owner. Alyssa informed me that every time Mr. Maxwell had a shipment of a new toy, he could be found playing with it all afternoon. We found Mr. Maxwell in a big vat of rainbow foam, which covered him from head to toe. Mr. Maxwell called to us to give him a minute and he would be right out. As soon as he opened the vat door, the rainbow foam disintegrated. He explained that the foam was edible. Once someone was inside, the foam came out in any color or design they desired. His personal favorite was the Tie-dye Swirl. The machine also had an array of flavors. To keep the kids healthy, the foam was low calorie plus low fat. He adored the flavor Broccoli Splendor."

Yuck! Everyone except for Joe and Angela thought.

"This isn't helping at all, is it?" Nana suddenly said, exasperated.

"It could lead to something, dear," Papa said, trying to encourage her.

"It soothes me, thinking of home," Joe said.

"I agree," Angela said.

"Besides, what else would we be doing right now if we weren't listening to your charming story?" Mr. Rupert stated.

Lina and Peter said simultaneously, "Tell us more."

Henry added politely, "Yes, please, I want to know more about the toy store!"

Nana smiled. "If you insist. Mr. Maxwell was a kind, eccentric, brilliant purple gumball Candonite. He smelled luscious, identical to grape juice. Soon Mr. Maxwell said that he needed to go do some actual work. The ride up to the second floor on melon-colored pogo sticks was a hoot. The level was dark, lit up by children playing with all kinds of toys that anyone could imagine playing with in the dark. Candonites ran by playing laser tag which was a game I wouldn't see again until years later in the 1980's. There were glow-in-the-dark darts twirling and spinning creating dazzling designs as they flew toward a glow-in-the-dark-target. I thought it had to be somewhat dangerous, running around playing in the dark with so many others doing the same. Alyssa stepped out in front of oncoming riders on glowing unicycles. I clenched my fists expecting a collision. Instead, Alyssa was still standing untouched after what should have been a terrible crash. The riders were still on their unicycles and no one was hurt. It was amazing! Like some sort of protective, invisible wall surrounding everyone."

Peter noted that Nana was now telling her story with her eyes open. *The memories must be coming easier to her now*, he thought.

"I was so thrilled to see a glow-in-the-dark drink bar," she continued. "Kids were sitting on glowing stools that rose up and down every time anyone sitting on one laughed. If you didn't want to spill your drink, you didn't laugh. For those who couldn't contain their laughter, a cleanup crew of glowing mechanical hands would quickly wipe up any mess. Alyssa ordered a cucumber frizz. I ordered a sarsaparilla drilla." The words rolled off Nana's tongue. "The cucumber fizz fizzed up the glass until Alyssa drank it down and it fizzed up again. My sarsaparilla drilla was served so cold the top of the drink was covered in a layer of ice and it came with a little drill. I looked over at Alyssa who was giggling, causing her stool to rise five feet up and back down. Alyssa pointed at the glass as she went up again. I drilled the top of my drink. The ice sheet shattered, dropping the pieces into my drink. It was cold, delicious, and refreshing."

"Bathroom break!" Henry shouted, loud enough to make nearly everyone jump. He disappeared down the hall.

Just as the bathroom door shut, the TV flashed on and Goaltan appeared.

Peter looked desperately around Goaltan's surroundings to see if he could recognize where he might be. It was no use. The cameraman's close-up on Goaltan was too tight.

"Lina Young, it seems your family isn't listed," Goaltan said, tearing a phone book in half with ease. "And Peter Fischer, it seems I hadn't been spelling your last name correctly." The cameraman panned out and Peter could see where Goaltan was standing.

Papa shot up to his feet. "My Sweet Shop!"

Goaltan walked to the doorway of Papa's Sweet Shop and held up the address card from Papa's Rolodex. "I will deal with this monstrosity," he said, pointing to the building. "And then, I am coming to your home, Peter, to make myself comfortable." He winked a devious wink which Peter knew was meant only for him.

"The address card! I left that out in the open, on the table!" Joe said, exasperated with himself.

Goaltan leaned toward the "Closed" sign that hung in the doorway of Papa's Sweet Shop. "Closed indeed!" he said, flicking the glass with his finger and sending a crack in slow motion up the glass in the door. Then he punched through the glass and grabbed the sign. Turning back to the camera, he snarled, "I'll keep this for a souvenir."

"I can't bear to watch," Nana said, her voice barely above a whisper.

"Turn it off!" Peter's mom pleaded.

"I can't," Peter said, pushing buttons on the remote.

"I'll unplug it," Mr. Rupert said, heading toward the TV. He pulled the plug just as Goaltan raised his hand above his head and laughed a horrible laugh. The TV went black.

Lina stated the obvious. "He is coming soon."

It remained quiet for a long moment, until Henry reappeared. "I'm hungry!" he complained.

Peter had been too preoccupied to notice until Henry mentioned it, but his stomach was also growling.

"We should keep up our energy," Peter's mom said, moving toward the kitchen.

Peter thought it didn't matter if anyone stood at the windows to keep watch. He had a feeling they would know when Goaltan was in the neighborhood.

"Can we hear more of the story now?" Henry asked politely.

Nana managed a soft smile. "I don't see why not." She inhaled a long breath to relax. "Mr. Maxwell really did save the best for last. The entry to the third floor was a brightly lit tunnel. At the end of that tunnel, I could see a little brownie Candonite with mint-green sprinkles holding a white ball in her hand. The girl grinned mischievously and threw the ball straight at my chest. As I took a step out of the tunnel, the wet ball hit me and splattered apart, falling to the ground. I looked up at the girl who was already running away giggling. Alyssa was giggling too. It was a snowball! Only this was no ordinary snowball! It wasn't cold and definitely wasn't nearly as wet as any other snowball I had been hit with before. I felt my clothes where the snowball had impacted. They were already dry. The vast room was covered in layers of white. It was peculiar that the air was quite cozy even with all of the snow."

Nana explained that Maple Town and Honey-ville always had warm sunny days. The Candonites learned about snow from humans and thought it was fascinating. They didn't have any of their own so Mr. Maxwell created the third floor. The area was huge, covered in snow with giant snow forts and elaborate ice treehouses. There was also an enormous bridge strung across the ceiling leading from treehouse to treehouse. The bridge consisted of different-sized snowflake crystals. There were two small hills and one very large hill for skiers, snowboarders, sleds, and even snowballers.

"What is a snowballer?" Henry asked with a mouth full of sandwich. Everyone had sandwiches. Some were only picking at their sandwiches, too nervous to eat.

Nana smiled. "I was getting to that part. A snowballer was a contraption invented by Mr. Maxwell. It was a ball big enough to fit up to four people inside facing each other. I watched as a group of Candonites boarded the ball and went rolling down the side of the snowy hill. It leaped right over skiers with ease and the riders inside squealed with delight. The third floor also contained an ice-skating rink which was located right in the middle of everything. A young, dashing Candonite man was performing figure eights and jumps above the ice."

Nana abruptly stopped telling her story as she heard the quiet neighborhood begin to stir. There was a low rumble and the floor beneath them shifted. Then it moved again and again. The lights flickered and soon after, the temperature in the room dropped. Goaltan was coming and he was very close.

Hidden Treasures

"It's time we got to movin'," Mr. Rupert said.

Everyone started to get up from the table. Then they suddenly realized that they had nowhere to move to.

"Follow me," Mr. Rupert said hastily. He didn't go very far. He stopped in the living room.

"What are we going to do?" Peter asked Lina, as if she would know. Lina shrugged her shoulders, as if she was disappointed that she didn't know.

"Everyone get to steppin' off the throw rug." Mr. Rupert got on his knees and kneeled in front of it.

Mrs. Young said, "A prayer now would be a good idea." She bowed her head and clasped her hands together.

Mr. Rupert brushed back the fringe of the rug and took a set of keys out of his pocket. With the tip of the key, he lifted up a very small piece of the wood floor, revealing a keyhole. Not everyone could see what he was doing.

"Shall I start the prayer?" Mrs. Young asked Mr. Rupert.

"Although that is a fantastic idea, I think it best we get into the cellar first." Mr. Rupert turned the key and lifted the rug, which was connected to part of the wooden floor, up above his head. A light revealed a winding staircase leading down.

"Wow, cool!" Henry exclaimed.

Peter thought it was cool too, but he was pretty sure Henry still had no idea what was really going on with Goaltan. *How nice it would be to be oblivious of worry, when your only concern was what toy you would play with next*, Peter thought.

"Now don't fret. There is plenty of room for everyone," Mr. Rupert said, waving them down the stairs.

Even though there were no windows, the spacious room at the bottom was well lit. Three walls were lined with mahogany wood shelves loaded with books. The wall with no books had coins hanging in frames. A door in that wall led to a small bathroom. A mahogany desk and small shelf next to it held more coins. The cluttered desk had a microscope, a magnifying glass, a few coins, scattered papers, and an open book that Peter was sure was a coin encyclopedia. There was also an old-time phone similar to one Peter had seen at a museum. Next to the phone was a picture of a young man who looked an awful lot like Mr. Rupert. A woman standing next to him held his hand and waved at the camera. Peter had been so preoccupied upstairs he hadn't looked at any pictures.

Peter thought the coolest part of the room was the mini-refrigerator next to the desk on the opposite side of the coin shelf. Peter always wanted a mini-refrigerator in his room, but that would never fly with his mother. A magazine rack sat between two love-seats. A frilly paisley couch faced the loveseats in the center of the room.

"This here is my treasure room, where I come to admire my coins and get some readin' done. Occasionally, I take a snooze in my chair. Make yourselves at home," Mr. Rupert told everyone.

There wasn't enough sitting room so Peter, Lina, Angela, and Joe sat on the floor. Henry walked over to the mini-fridge and opened the freezer door.

"Yum, ice cream sandwiches!" Henry said with delight.

"Henry, get out of there, right now!" Mrs. Young commanded.

"That's all right. I would be curious to know what was in that there fridge too," Mr. Rupert said, patting Henry on the head. "Ice cream sandwiches are my cravin'. I hid them in there. I doubt if ol' Goaltan will find them and I just can't bear to think of not eatin' my sandwiches. Let's see...grandtastic! There's enough for everyone!"

"Grandtastic?" Henry said.

"Oh yes, that is somethin' I made up," Mr. Rupert said, pointing to the picture on the desk. "That is my son and his lovely wife. I want to be a grandpa more than anythin'. My wife, rest her soul, wanted to be a grandma too. Whenever we would get around our son, we would use grandtastic instead of fantastic for any opportunity that the word seemed to fit. Sort of droppin' the hint we were still waitin' on those grandchildren. Hallelujah, I just found out last week that I am gonna be a grandpa!" The old man's eyes twinkled. Congratulations rang around the room.

"Can we have ice cream sandwiches, Ma?" Henry asked.

"No!" Lina and Peter answered in unison. They knew how Joe and Angela would feel about it. They were sure the Candonite children did not want to see everyone around them chomping down on something that might resemble their best friend or relative.

Mr. Rupert seemed to understand. "How about if it's okay with your mamma, you eat this one sittin' in my desk chair over in the corner so as to not disturb anyone." He waited for Mrs. Young's consent, then handed Henry the sandwich. He picked him up and put him in the desk chair, sliding the chair out of Joe and Angela's sight. He winked at the Candonite children and they smiled back.

"What else is in the fridge?" Henry asked as Mr. Rupert walked away.

"Just some orange juice, bread, and jam. My afternoon snack," Mr. Rupert answered.

"Do you get lonely down here?" Henry asked what Peter was thinking.

"Oh no, I have many friends there in the books I read. Old friends and new friends. I don't have time to be lonely. I am always on an adventure."

He picked up a book with a picture of a crimson jewel on the front off a shelf. "Right now, I am solvin' a high-profile mystery in Venice. My son also comes to visit with his wife every other week. They enjoy comin' down here and readin' books or comparin' our coin collections. My wife always wanted a hidden room ever since she read a book about one. I built her this here room and we hold our treasures in it." Mr. Rupert smiled.

"A secret room at my house would be awesome," Peter admitted.

"I would keep all my toys in my secret room so Lina couldn't play with them," Henry said.

"As if I play with your toys!" Lina protested.

"Do you have anything I would want to read?" Henry asked Mr. Rupert, ignoring Lina.

"Oh yes, I have a children's book section over here," Mr. Rupert said, leading Henry over to a shelf.

Henry started pulling books off the shelf, looking for the perfect one to read. All eyes except Nana's were on Henry. Peter thought, *It would be nice to be Henry at that moment, not a care in the world.* The room rumbled. One book fell sideways on a shelf and everyone near it jumped. Henry didn't seem to notice. He was busy jumping up and down because he had found one of his favorite books on the shelf.

"What is going on out there?" Mrs. Fischer questioned.

"I don't know and I ain't willin' to find out!"

Mr. Rupert answered, putting the book back in its place.

Everyone sat in silence for several minutes, just listening. Henry read his book to himself over and over. Nana, however, had her eyes closed. She was far away in Honeyville.

"We can't stay in here forever," Rod said.

"Yes, we can!" Mrs. Young said anxiously. Peter got the feeling she was worried her husband might try to go and investigate. Peter's mom must have gotten the same feeling too, because she asked Nana to continue telling about Honeyville. Maybe— just maybe—her story could possibly help.

As Nana resumed her story, she was inside Alyssa's family's limousine, sitting in the back seat with Alyssa's mother. Her mother was as beautiful as Alyssa. When the sun hit her just right, her light green candy crystals were almost blinding. The limo hovered a few feet off the ground and came with a chauffeur. They were approaching the family home. Nana described it as a mansion shaped like a colossal pyramid, turquoise in color with bright pink trim and a matching mailbox at the end of the long driveway.

"Once inside, Alyssa's mother informed us that dinner should be ready at any moment," Nana said. "Alyssa's father would not be joining us that night as he had a big dinner meeting. Alyssa told me that her father missed dinner all the time. She said her dad worked very hard to make sure her family had a good life. Alyssa would much rather have her dad at home for dinner every night and live in a rundown shack. The way Alyssa said it, I believed her. Alyssa's mother worked on inventions a couple of days a week in her lab at home. Her mom used to work until the wee hours of the morning until she realized that there were more important things in life."

"There certainly are," Mrs. Fischer interjected.

Nana continued, "At dinner, I was shocked to see the sparkling white floor graced with a spread fit for a party, yet only Alyssa's mother, Alyssa, and I were having dinner. There were lush pillows spread around the floor in luxurious rich fabrics. Alyssa's cat, which to my delight was a green version of one I had seen on a globe in the foyer, was a bundle of spearmint joy and sat on a pillow. As we enjoyed our meal, something remarkable happened to the dining room walls. Every five minutes or so, the pictures that adorned them would change. The colors of the walls would morph into the perfect shades that would match the pictures."

As Nana told her story, Peter observed the faces of his family and friends. Everyone looked like they were trying to enjoy Nana's pleasant tale, but there was no masking the worry on their faces. Peter had to do something. He couldn't stand to think what Goaltan was doing above ground. It wasn't fair that he was destroying the things Peter's family loved so deeply.

Flashes of Papa's Sweet Shop, Curtis Wheeler's mother's Cupcakery, and Happy's donut shop flickered in his sight. These people didn't deserve this. The house that Goaltan was seeking out was where Peter had grown up. He felt partially responsible. None of this would have happened if he hadn't gorged himself that fateful day, thereby transporting himself to Maple Town. Peter looked over at Lina. She sat with her legs crossed, twisting strands of carpet. Peter sensed she must have been thinking the same thing. His parents would never let him go above ground to face Goaltan. But it didn't matter; he knew in his heart what he had to do.

"I am going up there," he said, exhaling a deep breath. Peter wasn't sure where his newfound courage was coming from, but he was going to flow with it.

"I am going with you," Lina replied, standing up.

As Peter had expected, there was a chorus of disapproval.

"Look, I have to. I have to face Goaltan. We can't spend the rest of our lives down here," Peter said.

"He has a point there. We don't have enough chow to last us more than a couple days without going topside," Rod said.

"Dad, this isn't a submarine," Lina reminded him.

Rod managed a weak smile. "Sorry, it's the

military side of me."

"I guess some of us could take a look around. No promises of actually interacting with Goaltan, though," Peter's father said.

Not everyone agreed with this plan. However, ultimately the majority ruled. Peter and Lina received their wish.

Checking Things Out

The grownups decided that Peter, his dad, Lina, and her father, would go—as Rod had put it—topside. Nana would stay with Papa, continually looking for answers or help in her Honeyville journey. Mrs. Young would stay behind with Henry. Mr. Rupert and Peter's mom planned to head straight for the kitchen and storage closet for extra provisions and come right back down with the items they gathered. Joe and Angela were told to stay put as there was no telling what Goaltan would do if he found out about them.

Peter was the last one out the hatch door. Mr. Rupert started to close the door when he caught sight of Angela and Joe hustling up the stairs.

"We feel we can help too. We don't want to hide down there forever," Joe informed them.

Mr. Rupert pulled back the floorboards and let the Candonite children join them. Peter was pleasantly surprised and somewhat relieved at the additional help. Peter took into account that they had no plan. They just wanted to check out what they could find in a matter of minutes.

"Here," Joe said, placing something in Peter's hand. It was a small ceramic angel sculpture. The little angel was smiling, her head tilted, and holding one hand over her heart. Peter looked at Joe inquisitively.

"It's from Henry. He wanted you to have it. He said it would keep you safe. Henry isn't as oblivious as we thought." Joe smiled. Peter smiled back and placed the angel carefully in his pocket.

"Here we go, GI Joe," Lina whispered to Peter. He kind of liked that and gave her a nudge in return.

The first thing everyone did, besides Mr. Rupert and Peter's mom—who had their own agenda—was crowd around the windows and peek out the blinds. Peter glanced into the china cabinet and saw his own soldier action figure sitting in the place of where the little angel Henry gave him once sat. The soldier was positioned so that he had his hand over his heart. Peter smiled and squeezed the angel figurine in his pocket. Peering out the window, they saw nothing unusual. No sign of Goaltan and his goons. *What was he up to?* Peter thought. *Only one way to find out.*

Outside, Peter could feel his hands getting sweaty despite the unusual chill in the air. The cul-de-sac was eerily quiet. They all paired up to keep tabs on each other: Rod with Peter's dad, Angela with Joe, and Lina with Peter. Oddly, Peter felt the safest being paired with Lina. Perhaps it had something to do with the fact that they had already been on a quest together into Goaltan's territory. Peter felt more confident moving stealthily next to his best friend. They were a team, a force to be reckoned with.

No sign of Goaltan. No sign of the Peblars. *It couldn't be that hard to find his house,* Peter thought. *After all, Goaltan did have the address. What was taking him so long? Perhaps he had to find a map. Perhaps he had to stop to eat. Perhaps he wasn't coming at all.*

A violent rumble shook the ground and Lina lost her footing, stepping on Peter's foot.

He reacted with a low "Ow!"

"Sorry," Lina replied, just as low.

Everyone within sight was staying close to concealing objects like a tree, a car, and a garbage can. Peter couldn't see his father or Rod. A piercing whistling noise echoed nearby.

Lina gestured forward to all who could see. "Let's check it out."

Peter, Lina, Joe, and Angela ventured forward. No time to worry about where Rod and Mr. Fischer went. The obvious thing to do was move toward the entrance of the cul-de-sac to see down the intersecting street.

"We'll take the opposite side of the street," Joe said. Peter watched as both his friends, one brilliant yellow and one rainbow-chipped, dashed away.

"We better hurry too," Peter suggested to Lina, who was looking around for the first time and noticed her dad and Peter's dad were missing. She grabbed Peter's hand and guided him from house to house until they were at the end of the cul-de-sac. Angela and Joe were already crouching behind a fence on the opposite side of the street. Lina gasped and Peter swallowed hard when three Peblars captured Rod and Peter's dad, taking them hostage. Rod was yelling something the children couldn't quite make out.

"Dad!" Lina whispered desperately.

Peter had one immediate response, to grab Lina and pull her behind a parked car. They watched as the Peblars shoved their dads into the lavender Cupcakery delivery truck. The truck was shaped in the form of a cupcake with chocolate sprinkles and a strawberry on top. It was a strange choice for a holding cell. Peter was surprised the Peblars hadn't destroyed it. *Where were they taking them?* Peter wondered. He and Lina watched in horror as two other Peblars reached over the fence, grabbed Joe and Angela, heaved them effortlessly over the fence and pulled them toward the truck. *Oh spam!*

Peter realized he was squeezing the door handle of a parked car. He stared down at his knuckles, which had turned white. He tried the door handle, relieved it was unlocked. The dark tinted windows would aid in concealing them.

"Get in," Peter whispered to Lina. They climbed into the car hastily and shut the door silently. They watched as the Peblars locked Angela and Joe in the back of the truck with the others. *What now?* The ground rumbled again and the car swayed with every sound. More Peblars were joining the party, coming from all sides. Goaltan was not hard to make out amongst them. He was the biggest, brawniest, and meanest looking of them all. Peter realized that in that moment, Goaltan was the one he feared the most.

Peter and Lina were relieved to see that the truck stayed put and did not go speeding away. However, two stout Peblars leaned against the doors, guarding the prisoners.

"We don't have much time before they find your house," Lina said.

"I know," Peter answered glumly.

"We have to do something!" Lina said with desperation, reaching for the door handle of the car.

"Stop!" Peter said, barely above a whisper. "You can't go off and get yourself caught too. What good would that do?"

"I suppose you are right," Lina agreed.

Peter noticed Goaltan and his crew heading toward them. In the background, the Cupcakery truck rocked back and forth, evidence of his friends trying to escape. With every step, Goaltan seemed to be getting angrier, sensing he was closing in on Peter's home. Goaltan's feet came down hard on the asphalt as soon as he reached the street Peter lived on. Peter and Lina ducked down as they saw the asphalt crack beneath his feet. Even through the car they could smell the rancid beasts. Their noses wrinkled in response.

The children could hear the Peblars approaching and Goaltan's sinister laughter vibrated the car windows. Shortly after, a thunderous thud came from above Peter's and Lina's heads. It took everything they had not to react. They waited as they heard the Peblars pass the car. Slowly they looked up and saw that Goaltan had left an imprint of his fist dented into the roof of the car. The children gulped.

Peter dropped his head in his hands. "If we don't do something soon, my neighborhood will be destroyed."

"They always say this in the movies, so I will give it a try….Everything is going to be all right," Lina said, trying to lighten the mood.

Peter lifted his head and gave her a grimace. "I don't know if this will work, but I am going to try talking with Goaltan."

"Are you loony tunes?" Lina wrinkled her nose up at him.

"I have to try reasoning with him. Are you coming with me?" Peter hesitated with his hand on the door handle.

"Well, I am not letting you go alone," Lina answered with a soft smile.

Redecorating

Peter was thankful to have his friend by his side. He inhaled deeply then exhaled as he opened the door. Goaltan had reached Peter's driveway and was holding something in his hand.

"My mailbox!" Peter shouted, his voice trembling, his face burning with fear and anger.

Goaltan swung around at the sound of Peter's voice.

"This is the least of your worries!" Goaltan said, tossing the mailbox into the air. It landed a few inches from Peter's and Lina's feet, causing them to cringe and stumble backwards. Goaltan and his goons found this quite humorous. Their raucous laughter echoed through the neighborhood.

"Are you here to surrender or did you just come to watch me destroy your humble abode?" Goaltan toyed with Peter, lifting his right foot up a few inches and slamming it back down into Peter's driveway, making a miniature crater.

"Stop!" Peter replied. "I am here, aren't I? That is what you wanted."

"Yes, yes," Goaltan answered. "I suppose, but demolishing things suits me well." The Peblars snickered and Peter and Lina could also hear voices coming from behind them. They were surrounded by the pebbled enemy.

"You don't need to demolish anything else. We get the message. What do you want with us?" Lina asked.

Goaltan strolled toward the children. "I'll tell you what I want. I would like very much to stay here and make this town my new home. I have grown tired of my own land and your world is splendidly fun! Of course, a little makeover will have to take place," Goaltan said, glancing around the cul-de-sac. "I think I will make your particular home"—he paused for dramatic effect—"mine!" A sinister smile spread across his lips. "Peter, Lina, and your two little Candonite friends shall be my own personal servants. Or should I say, slaves?"

"I'll never lift a finger for you!" Lina scowled as Goaltan came to a stop in front of them.

"Oh, I think you will change your mind. It all comes down to whether or not you want your fathers to go free and be with the rest of your families. Or shall I make them my servants too? Hmmm," Goaltan said playfully.

"You're horrible!" Lina replied, crossing her arms.

"You have hurt my feelings," Goaltan mused. "I could have said I will keep you all to serve me. Don't forget that."

"I—" Lina started to reply but Peter touched her arm and interrupted her.

"We would be grateful if you left our families out of this." He whispered to Lina. "Think of Henry." She pursed her lips. Peter turned his attention back to Goaltan and said, "I will be your greatest servant if you let everyone else go."

"You are not going to do this without me," Lina told Peter.

"Such loyalty," Goaltan replied, considering the offer. "You would risk your freedom to help...him?"

"Of course! Peter is my friend. My best friend," Lina answered. "He would do the same thing for me."

"I would," Peter confirmed.

"Oh, how heartwarming," Goaltan said sarcastically. "Friends! Who needs friends? I have never had a friend in my life and I turned out fine." He sneered. Peter and Lina wanted to reply, but thought it best not to. Lina bit her lower lip to keep from saying anything.

"Do you accept the offer of having us serve you and letting our families and friends go?" Peter asked, his voice breaking.

"I don't make deals with children, especially not human children. If I made that deal, I would always have to watch my back looking for your pesky family. Who, no doubt, would attempt to rescue you," Goaltan huffed.

Peter and Lina were about to protest his answer when suddenly Goaltan stomped his foot. They felt the earth under them shake. The asphalt around them rose rapidly toward the sky. The ring of asphalt carried Lina and Peter two stories up before coming to an abrupt stop. Peter and Lina lost their balance. Peter fell onto his backside and Lina fell sideways with her legs and torso dangling over the side of the asphalt ring. Peter rushed to her side to help her up.

"Sheesh! Seriously, what is with the dramatic effects?" she yelled down to Goaltan, furious and panting.

Goaltan returned a deafening laugh. "I can't risk your running off while I take care of business, can I? Just sit back and enjoy the show."

"What are you going to do?" Peter demanded, angry that his best friend could have gotten hurt.

Goaltan didn't answer. Instead he did a little jig and pivoted around, heading toward Peter's home. The other Peblars followed him. Peter and Lina watched powerlessly. As soon as Goaltan grabbed the handle of Peter's front door, the house began to slowly turn gray. Tiny pebbles began replacing the wooden walls. Goaltan watched for a moment, no doubt pleased with his work, before crushing the doorknob in his bare hand.

Before entering, Goaltan turned to the children and spoke. His voice, startlingly loud as if he spoke right into their ears, caused them to cringe. "I don't think you will be going anywhere anytime soon. All this reconstruction makes one weary. It is time for me to get some much needed rest. I think I will rest my head on your pillow."

Peter wanted to protest but Goaltan was already entering the door. He turned his body to fit into the doorway, ducked to clear the top frame and failed, taking part of it off as he slammed the door shut behind him. Peter couldn't get a word out. Peter and Lina watched, upset with the house taking on its new form. Some of the Peblars went into the house. A couple stayed in front standing guard. Two more made their way around to the back of the house.

"What now?" Lina asked.

"People keep asking that question and no one seems to have the answer," Peter replied.

"Yeah, I know," Lina said glumly.

"Try not to look at Mr. Rupert's house. We don't want to draw any attention to it," Peter advised.

"This stinks!" Lina said. Although he agreed, Peter didn't answer. As if things couldn't get any worse, he felt a raindrop on the tip of his nose, then another on his cheek.

"You have got to be kidding me!" Lina said, holding out her hands toward dark clouds in the sky. Peter hadn't noticed those clouds before, because he had been so busy paying attention to Goaltan and his crew.

He attempted to be optimistic. "Maybe it will just drizzle."

Lina gave him a look that meant, "Yeah, right!"

The downpour started. It wouldn't have been

so bad if it wasn't freezing. The rain seemed to fall from all directions. No matter which way they turned, their faces were pelted with the frosty drops. Before long, the Peblars must have tired of the rain. Dripping wet, they made their way inside Peter's house. Peter couldn't help thinking what his mother would have said about that: "Oh no you don't, you'll wipe yourself down with a towel first!"

"They know we aren't going anywhere," Peter said over the noise of the rain.

Those words did something to Lina. Peter wasn't sure at first. *Could she be crying?* But he knew that Lina never cried. Not even when he saw her smashed in the face with a soccer ball at the last field day. Peter was sure he would have at least shed a tear. It left a welt on her forehead until the next morning and a bruise for a week. But here she was softly crying and Peter knew exactly how she felt.

"It is going to be all right, Lina. It has to be." Peter made the attempt to wipe her tears away from her face as best as he could through the rain.

"I am soooooo incredibly mad. And, well, a little bit scared," Lina admitted, wiping what Peter thought was the last of her tears away with the back of her hand.

"I know," Peter answered, managing a weak smile. "Me too."

They sat in silence for what seemed forever. The two of them were unpleasantly cold to the point that they almost didn't notice the annoying drops anymore. "It would be nice to see the sun," Lina whispered.

Peter nodded. Regardless of the cold, he felt extremely tired and his eyelids grew heavy. He fought the need to close them for as long as he could, but it was no use. His eyelids won. Soon Peter was dreaming.

Peter liked this dream very much. He was with Nana and they were standing in lush blue-green grass. Trees that seemed to be pointing stood nearby. A pair of marshmallow birds flew past overhead and Peter knew without a doubt that he was in Maple Town. A warm feeling swept over him and he smiled from ear to ear. From a distance, he saw a peppermint cat come strolling along. It rubbed up against his leg like it had the first time Peter arrived in Maple Town. Nana bent down and picked up the cat and stroked it while the cat seemed to be purring a little song. It was peaceful to be standing there now, so far away from Goaltan. It wasn't as warm as usual and Peter did notice it smelled a bit off, not as pleasantly fragrant as usual. The sky above was darkening and Peter felt a raindrop fall on his forearm. Something wasn't right. It never rained in Maple Town.

"There you two are!" came a booming voice. Peter and Nana looked in its direction. Goaltan was rapidly approaching them. *Goaltan in Maple Town, how was this possible?* Peblars stormed the hillside behind Goaltan. Peter grabbed Nana's arm and attempted to pull her along. She wasn't budging despite his efforts. Goaltan was almost to them.

"Nana!" Peter shouted desperately.

Peter's eyes shot open and he awoke from his dream. Seconds later, his front door swung open and out came a Peblar to check the weather. The Peblar shouted back into the house and soon two of them were tossing Peter's mailbox back and forth across the lawn like a football.

"Grrrrrrr!" Lina said under her breath.

Peter sighed.

Lina turned with a huff to face away from the football players. Peter studied the unfamiliar scene of his home.

Within an hour, Goaltan was standing in front of the doorway stretching. He was so massive that when his arms were stretched above his head he reached the second-story window. Peter imagined Goaltan napping in his bed with his humongous feet dangling off the edge. It made Peter cringe.

"Such a nice nap," Goaltan boomed. "A comfy bed you have there, Peter. Upon settling in, I may have broken it. Oh well."

Lina turned around to see Peter's anger spreading through his body. His fists were clenched in spite of how frozen they must have been.

"Leave us alone!" Her voice broke.

"As you wish!" Goaltan beamed a sinister smile as he tapped his right foot to the ground in an exaggerated movement.

"Not again!" Peter said as he felt the asphalt beneath him tremble. Faster than a blink, a crack split the asphalt right down the middle, separating Peter and Lina before they even had a chance to think about what was happening. They were now twenty feet apart. Luckily, Lina was still sitting or she would have been knocked to the ground. Peter shuddered at the thought. Lina stood up.

"You should watch what you ask for, my dear," Goaltan snickered.

Lina opened her mouth to say something and Goaltan raised his foot again. Lina reluctantly closed her mouth and Goaltan set his foot back down to a relaxed position. She looked at the ground, defeated. Peter stared back at her. He suddenly felt incredibly lonely.

Goaltan walked over to the garage. "What is in here?" he said as he peeled the door upward like a tuna can with one hand. Goaltan pulled out Papa's moped with little effort. He pondered for a moment before he mounted it. The weight was too much for the little bike to handle. The tires burst and the sound of crushing metal was almost unbearable for Peter's ears as he watched his Papa's bike being smashed to pieces.

"Oops," Goaltan said casually. "I think I will stick to the old-fashioned way of travel, by foot."

Peter ground his teeth, but said nothing.

"Well, I am off to do some more interior and exterior decorating of your little town. Don't worry, I won't be long. I have to decide what I will have you two do for me first." Goaltan whistled and soon Peblars started filing out of the house to follow him as he moved down the street between Lina and Peter. A few Peblars stayed behind to stand guard.

A Gift from the Garden

About an hour passed. Peter and Lina watched helplessly as the neighborhood began to look more and more unfamiliar. Gray pebbles replaced the houses, mailboxes, fences, everything that wasn't growing. Those things that were growing like trees, grass, and flowers were gradually turning the same dull gray color and withering, an ocean of darkness forming around them.

Peter thought about his family and friends separated from each other and couldn't bear to think about how long that would last. Peter thought about how he wished he was curled up on Nana's comfy floral couch, listening to her tell more stories of Honeyville. Peter wondered if he would ever be able to hear the rest of that story. He thought about how cold it was. He thought about what his best friend might be thinking about. He thought about what Goaltan's first task might be for them. Peter thought about so many different things.

In the midst of all his thinking, Nana came walking briskly down the sidewalk toward Peter, holding something in her hands.

"What are you doing, Nana?" Peter screamed as she raced toward him. He could see that she was gripping a large pot with two potholders.

"I don't have much time, Peter," she said. They shot glances toward the two Peblars, who had just noticed her.

"Run, Nana!" Peter shouted.

"Listen closely, Peter," Nana said.

Peter nodded, glancing again at the Peblars who were striding toward them.

"Goaltan exists because of fear," Nana managed to say before the Peblars were upon her, practically growling through their teeth. She lifted the pot lid and instantly the two Peblars relaxed, looking more like doe-eyed deer than mean, rotted Cadonites.

"How about some nice hot vegetable soup? Straight from garden to kitchen." Nana smiled pleasantly, wafting the scent of the soup toward the Peblars with the lid. "Warms you right up on a day like this. If you show me some manners, there is more where this came from."

The Peblars looked at each other and then back at Nana and the precious bounty she carried. They gestured to her to lead the way. Peter thought that vegetable soup sounded magnificent to him right now. It must have been that much more appealing to the Peblars.

Nana shot a look back up at Peter and gave him a reassuring smile to let him know she was okay. She led the way back to Peter's house. The other Peblars who were outside fell in line, following

Nana into the house.

What did Nana mean? Goaltan exists because of fear? Peter already knew Goaltan was feared by all. That wasn't anything new.

"What was that all about?" Lina called to him.

"I'm not sure," Peter answered truthfully.

Before he had time to analyze it, Goaltan returned, his presence already felt before they could see him. He was laughing, as if he was pleased with himself. The asphalt beneath Peter and Lina swayed as Goaltan approached.

Peter could only think about one thing now, and that was Nana. Goaltan already had his father, Ron, Angela, Joe, and his best friend Lina. He didn't want Goaltan to add Nana to his collection too.

"Oh, still hanging out, are we?" Goaltan said slyly, as if Peter and Lina had a choice to be elsewhere at the moment.

Peter and Lina made no comment.

"You want to know something quite wonderful?" Goaltan asked the children. Without waiting for their answer he continued. "I have discovered that my powers are even greater than ever before in this world. This place is simply magnificent!" He beamed.

"Without those powers you wouldn't be so tough," Lina snapped.

"I see you want a demonstration!" Goaltan replied.

"That isn't what I said!" Lina barked back.

With his elbow bent, Goaltan raised his finger to the sky and winked snidely at Lina. A bolt of lightning flashed down toward the ground below Lina's raised asphalt, obliterating the earth and leaving a gaping hole. Lina and Peter were still shielding their eyes from the lightning a minute after the strike. In the background, they heard Goaltan chuckling. Peter wasn't sure if he wanted to uncover his eyes when he finally could. He didn't want to look at Goaltan and see the yellows of his eyes.

"Thanks for the demonstration," Peter said sarcastically. He didn't mean to say anything. It simply slipped out of his mouth and as soon as he said it, Peter wished he could take it back.

"You would like to see more, would you?" Goaltan said, amused.

Peter didn't bother replying. He knew Goaltan would show them regardless.

"I remember I left my sign I obtained from a newly remodeled candy shop on a basketball hoop back that way. I'll be back in a jiff," Goaltan said as he bent down to push a section of asphalt forward. It spread upwards, creating a sky bridge that formed above houses, telephone poles, everything in its path. Goaltan stepped on the sky bridge and headed away to find the sign. He soon returned with it in hand. Peter groaned at the sight of Papa's sign.

"I'm famished! Remodeling is hard work. My first task for you, Peter and Lina, is to cook me a meal fit for a king. This is my new kingdom! And I am your king!" Goaltan declared.

Peter expected Lina to have something to say about that. However, she said nothing. Instead she stared at her feet.

"I have yet to think of the first task for your friends in the truck. I am sure they are quite cozy and can wait a bit longer. If you two mind me, this little arrangement could work out quite nicely. If not, I could always make these asphalt pedestals beneath your feet permanent homes," Goaltan warned.

Peter remembered Nana inside and didn't want Goaltan to discover her. He didn't want another one of his loved ones serving King Pebble Brain. He wished he was close enough to Lina to whisper the pebble brain part in her ear. His mother didn't like him saying negative things about other people, but he was pretty sure in this instance she wouldn't mind.

Before Peter comprehended what was happening, Goaltan threw the sign toward the lawn. He then jumped up a few inches off the ground and instantly the asphalt beneath them plummeted toward the street below. Peter and Lina nosedived toward Goaltan. Before they became one with the pavement, Goaltan grabbed them by their ankles, their noses dangling an inch from the ground.

Peter and Lina were still screaming when Goaltan said, "No need to thank me for helping you down!" He walked toward Peter's house, still holding them by their ankles.

Was this to be his life from now on? Peter thought. *Waiting on Goaltan and the Peblars for everything they desired? What had Nana meant by "Goaltan exists because of fear"?*

Heads Up!

Peter thought about the way Nana had bravely spoken to the Peblars and walked side by side with them. He concentrated on the memory. He remembered that Nana actually looked pretty relaxed, considering the Peblars could have done almost anything to her. *Was that the key, show Goaltan no fear? But how would that be possible? Goaltan is so strong and powerful and I am just not any of those things.* Peter's thoughts were interrupted when Goaltan rolled Lina and Peter onto the once-green lawn.

"Ouch! That was uncalled for," Lina said, dusting herself off and getting up.

Peter had a handful of gray dirt and could feel it beneath his fingertips. He thought to himself that he wouldn't wash his hands before preparing Goaltan's meal. Peter opened his hand and let the dirt escape from it as he stood, knowing he would only make things worse if Goaltan discovered it in his food. It was then he realized that in moments Nana would be discovered.

Goaltan continued toward the door, not bothering to look back at Peter and Lina. He was too powerful now to worry that they might try to escape.

A flick of his finger and his prey would be caught. Goaltan's hand was on the doorknob and he began turning it.

Peter's stomach muscles tightened and his head was pounding from all the thinking. Suddenly Peter understood Nana's words. Without any conscious thought, Peter blurted out, "I may have gotten to Maple Town by a bellyache, but your coming to my town has given me a headache. It is time for you to go home!"

Peter was shocked at his own words and the fact that he said them with such force and confidence. He supposed Lina was shocked too when he saw that her mouth was open wide enough to fit a baseball inside. Goaltan didn't move from his position at the door. A moment passed before he slowly turned to face Peter with an unreadable expression.

"What did you say?" Goaltan said, in a soft warning voice.

Peter mustered up his courage and said, "I am not afraid of you!"

Goaltan snarled, "I do not believe you."

Peter turned to Lina and whispered, "Nana said he exists because of fear. My guess is without our fear he would be powerless." *It must be true because Goaltan hasn't smashed me to oblivion yet,* he thought.

"I am not afraid of you either! You're nothing but a big bully!" Lina said firmly.

By this time, crowds of Peblars had gathered at the windows. The door opened. Nana stood in the doorway in front of a Peblar.

"Oh, you're not afraid, are you? We'll just see about that!" Goaltan shouted, lifting his foot off the ground and stomping it as hard as he could. He swirled up dust but nothing else happened. Peter and Lina took a step closer to each other. Still nothing happened.

Nana clapped her hands together in triumph. The Peblars inside watched from the windows and door, dumbfounded. Goaltan grew angrier. He raised his finger furiously toward the sky and narrowed his eyes. Still nothing. Goaltan growled as he grabbed the edge of the house and tried with all his might to crush it. When that didn't work, he tried kicking it and ended up stubbing his toe. A large pebble broke off the house and hit him in the eye. Goaltan yelped noisily, almost fearfully.

When he regained his composure, he approached Peter and Lina. "Well, I guess I have to do this the old-fashioned way, with my bare hands!"

The children took one another's hands. They weren't planning to budge. All of a sudden, the special delivery box dropped directly onto Goaltan's head. It tumbled, flaps open, onto the ashy dried-up grass. To Peter, it looked like the same box that he had seen the day he visited Maple Town, the same box that brought Lina and him home from Maple Town, the same box that brought Angela and Joe to them, and the same box that brought Goaltan here. Out of the box flowed frosty air laced with a terrible stench.

"What is this?" Goaltan demanded.

Peter watched the red "Special Delivery" letters on the box light up and he answered Goaltan confidently, "This is your ticket out of here!"

"I don't think so!" Goaltan said as he lunged toward Peter.

Goaltan was within inches of reaching Peter when the box lashed forward and swallowed him whole in one smooth speedy motion. There was a loud strained gulping noise. The Peblars inside Peter's home began to disperse, some running outside and some hiding inside. But they couldn't hide. A great gust of wind sucked them into the box, one by one. Despite the heavy winds, Peter, Lina, and Nana remained upright with little more than a few hairs blowing out of place.

For the remaining Peblars, however, it was a different story. They were flying down the street from the Cupcakery truck. The wind was so strong that their feet weren't touching the ground. The Peblars weren't going gracefully either. They were flailing their arms and legs all the way. One Peblar thought he could hold onto the side of the house but he lost that battle quickly.

When the wind began to die down and the atmosphere seemed to be settling, it unexpectedly picked back up and Peter saw a very short Peblar floating down the road. The Peblar was chomping down on some carrots with the leaves still attached. Oblivious to what was going on, the Peblar suddenly disappeared into the box. A moment later, the half-eaten carrots shot back out of the box and landed in front of Lina's feet.

"Gross!" she said.

Peter laughed. Lina replied by sticking her tongue out at him. Peter smiled back. The wind stirred back up, coming even louder and faster, blowing their hair this way and that as it swirled and twirled, sucking in pebbles from every direction and working to repair its surroundings.

When Peter, Lina, and Nana started to see green grass again they all cheered. Peter's house was beginning to look like his home again. The sky cleared and the air lost its rancid smell. Everyone took deep breaths. It was nice to breathe the familiar air again. Warmth returned promptly. The wind stopped when most of what Goaltan had done was cleared. The special delivery box sat unmoving, the letters still glowing neon red.

They heard familiar voices coming from down the street. Peter's father, Rod, Angela, and Joe all ran gleefully toward them. Peter noticed the street had not been completely repaired. He knew that meant some of Goaltan's destruction would remain. Peter thought about Papa's Sweet Shop, Happy Donuts, and other places that may have been destroyed. He would have to worry about all that later, because

Peter saw his mother, Mr. Rupert, Mrs. Young, Henry, and other neighbors emerging from homes now and he was too overjoyed.

People's mouths were agape when they saw the two Candonites running merrily toward Peter's house. Peter, Lina, and Nana ran toward them. The special delivery box followed slowly behind them, floating slightly above the ground. Peter had a feeling he knew why. The box would give him enough time to say goodbye to his friends before it would return them safely home. Peter was suddenly sad. He didn't want to say goodbye again, even though he knew he had to. Everyone was staring at the Candonite children while they were cheering.

Peter spoke first. "Nana was right. Goaltan couldn't stay here if I stopped being afraid of him—if I showed him no fear."

"You were all so brave!" Peter's mother said.

"How did you know what to do, Nana?" Peter asked.

"That evening I spent with Alyssa's family, her father eventually came home and told us a story before bedtime. That particular night, he happened to tell a story of a Candonite man who had been banished long ago for his treatment of others and their belongings. That man was Goaltan. Alyssa told me it was a true story and I had no reason to doubt her. Especially when she revealed information her father did not share. Alyssa told me that she was related to Goaltan. She wasn't supposed to know but she had overheard a conversation. It was a family secret no one wanted to admit to."

"Who would?" Lina said.

"That night I had a dream. I was standing somewhere very dark and cold, and I felt so alone. I called out for my mother, my father, and even Alyssa. But none of them came. Instead, I heard a low chuckle that sent a pang of fear through my entire body. I couldn't tell where the chuckle was coming from but I knew it was very close. I was desperately looking around for a way to escape but it was so dark I couldn't tell which way to go. The chuckle was getting louder and my instincts were to back up. I soon backed into a wall and began to feel my way out, all the while the chuckle rising to an unruly laugh. I began to panic. Suddenly, I heard a voice—Alyssa's voice. She said, 'He thrives off of fear; he exists because you fear him. He cannot harm you if you are not afraid.' Upon waking from the nightmare, I had a gut feeling that someday I would need this information. Today, I knew the information was meant for you, Peter."

Peter had all but forgotten about the box until it nudged his right shoulder as if to remind him his friends needed to be on their way. The top flaps of the box unfolded and warm sweet air filled his nostrils.

"I guess that is our cue to say our goodbyes," Angela said with a small laugh.

"I guess so," Peter chuckled.

"It was a pleasure," Joe said, smiling and leaning forward to exchange hugs with Peter and Lina.

"We will remember you, always," Angela said.

"And we will remember you too," Lina replied.

"Say hello to Poke, the Bakers, everyone for me," Peter said. He smiled, remembering the friends he had made in Maple Town just days before. Yet it seemed so long ago after all he had been through.

"We will," Joe replied.

The special delivery box tilted forward to let them know it was time. Angela and Joe nodded that they were ready and the box inched forward and a warm familiar gust of air surrounded them, the fragrant scent of the Candonites' home. There was no sign of Goaltan and the Peblars now, just a peaceful atmosphere inviting them home. Angela and Joe waved one final time before the box swallowed them. It finished with the usual gulp and disappeared. There were gasps and excited murmurs from the neighbors and laughter from Henry, who was sitting on the curb happily reading one of Peter's comic books. Peter, his friends, and family laughed too.

Meteors and Martians

"I can't believe the latest news! People are saying the damage to the town was caused by meteorites. That is crazy!" Peter said to Lina, holding up a newspaper as he sat on his front porch three months later.

"Oh, and saying a bunch of pebbled beasts came and destroyed the town trying to rid it of all delectable confections would be much more believable." Lina grinned, snatching the newspaper out of Peter's hands to take a look.

"I guess I see your point," Peter replied, looking toward the repaired street before him.

Lina giggled. "My favorite is still the theory of the gray Martians from outer space."

Peter chuckled.

"I don't think I told you this yet, but I was thinking it. You look...nice," he said carefully.

"Thanks. I feel a little silly. My mother made my outfit for me. She practically cried when I told her I wouldn't wear it. So, of course, I had to wear it. It's called a *baro't saya*, a traditional Filipino dress shirt and skirt."

"Well, you don't look silly," Peter said.

"Thanks. You don't look silly either," Lina

replied.

"Thanks," Peter said, as he stood up and straightened his tie.

Peter's mother opened the door. "You two ready to go? We don't want to be late."

"Yep, we just have to pick up Henry on the way," Peter replied.

Everyone in town would be dressed to impress royalty today. It was "Unveiling Day." Everyone was talking about it everywhere they went.

Mr. Rupert, his son and daughter-in-law, Buddy and Lisa Rupert, came out of the house. Henry was in the garden. He skipped to the SUV holding a paper cup in his hand. Once Henry was inside he slid up close to Lina, almost hugging her, and said charmingly, "I have something for you."

"What is it?" Lina asked.

Henry held it up real close under her nose. "A worm."

Lina practically cracked heads with Peter trying to back away from the slimy little creature. "Yuck, Henry! Like I really want a worm!"

"You did say you wanted to start a collection of your own of something that no one else has. Well, who collects worms?" Henry said.

"Oh, Henry. What am I going to do with you?" Lina sighed.

Mr. Rupert cleared his throat as if he had something very important to say. "I am so excited I could spit!" Mr. Rupert said as he slapped the side of his leg. "My son and his pretty li'l wife are movin' into town. Only minutes away from me!"

"That's grandtastic!" Peter replied and everyone agreed.

"A good job opened up and we found a great deal on a house in town," Buddy said.

"We better get to scootin'! I could talk about this all night. But we all have an agenda now, don't we?" Mr. Rupert gave a cheerful wink and scurried off.

Signs throughout town read "UNVEILING DAY!" Reporters and news crews gathered in front of the new building Curtis's mother and Happy had combined forces to create. They met up with Nana, Papa, and Lina's parents at the ribbon cutting. Papa had ridden in on his new moped, the exact color and model of his last one.

Mr. Rupert made the opening speech. "I am so deeply touched to get to cut this here ribbon and open the goody shop. As y'all know, the Cupcakery and Happy Donuts have collaborated to bring the sweetest thing...Happy Donuts Cupcakery! The only place for miles around where you can get a donut that looks like a tasty cupcake. So everybody get to samplin' the goods!" Mr. Rupert cut the shimmery red ribbon. Camera flashes sparked like the Fourth of July.

Peter couldn't believe it when he heard the news that Mr. Rupert had sold an extremely rare coin from his collection and gave the money to

Happy, Mrs. Wheeler, and Papa to help rebuild their shops. Mr. Rupert explained, "I really don't need anythin' else. I have new wonderful friends, a lovin' son and daughter-in-law, and a grandbaby fixin' to be born. What more could this lucky old man want?"

Mr. Rupert was no longer "old man Rupert." Now he was simply Mr. Rupert, a really nice man.

Peter and Lina were bombarded by serving trays filled with little donut cupcakes topped with sprinkles and frosting. They each took one and popped it in their mouths. *Yum*, Peter thought. A waitress came by, decked out in cupcake garb from head to toe. Charming frosted glass tabletops that had sprinkles beneath a layer of glass and cupcake-designed chairs really brought the shop to life.

The Sweetest Sweet Shop

Papa's Sweet Shop was the grand finale of the day. Peter knew that the sweet shop would be outrageous. It was his idea, after all, to have a piece of Maple Town and Honeyville in his very own town.

Peter worked diligently on the details with Papa. Papa wanted everything to be an awe-inspiring surprise. Peter remembered in the beginning stages when he had heard the heartbreaking whispers of his parents talking about the damage done by Goaltan. Now, everything was really going to be okay.

The building was bigger than the original Papa's Sweet Shop, standing two stories instead of one. The sweet shop looked scrumptious, with replica candies and treats ornamenting the chocolaty colored building.

Papa squeezed Peter's shoulders and whispered in his ear, "We get to go inside first before anyone else!"

Peter and Lina raced inside. Papa closed the doors behind them, pulling on the peppermint handles and pointing out the sign from the old shop, a reminder that Goaltan's plans had failed. No one spoke.

The floors were reminiscent of the ones in

Maple Town, resembling shimmering iridescent candy wrappers. There was an orange twisty slide that started on the second floor. In the center of the shop there was a crystal rock candy elevator. Every table was a larger replica of the open special delivery box; the flaps of the box made up the table top. The center of the table top was a glowing light covered by glass.

"Do you like it, Peter?" Papa asked.

Peter hugged his grandpa. "Like it? I more than like it. I more than love it! There are no words!"

Peter turned his attention to the back wall. "Hover cars!"

"Climb aboard," Papa said.

Peter and Lina entered the car doors and slid in on opposite sides of a table. An electronic voice said, "Please fasten your seatbelt and enjoy the wild treats from the sweetest place you'll ever eat, Papa's Sweet Shop!" Lina repeated the slogan, practically singing it. A glove compartment was marked "MENUS." Peter pulled out a menu printed to look like a road map.

There was a special section of the menu marked "Candonite Delights." The items included Satisfying Spinach Pie, Vegetating Veggie Soup served with a side of Corny Corn Soufflé, Amazing Avocado Gazpacho, and a few more would-be Candonite favorites.

"Just in case our friends are ever in the neighborhood again," Papa said. He winked and pushed his glasses back on the bridge of his nose. Papa told them that Peter's dad, Mr. Rupert, and even Lina's mother would be working there.

"Really?" Peter and Lina said excitedly.

On the top floor, a wooden hostess podium with menus on both sides was directly in front of them. Words carved into the wood to appear like lightening had struck the podium read "Weather Extremes at Papa's."

Papa led the children to the frosted glass door on the right. As soon as he opened it, frigid air touched their skin. Papa went over to a long rack full of multiple-sized fur-lined coats that all had a Papa's Sweet Shop logo on them. He pulled off one for each child and one for himself.

"This is wild!" Lina said.

"It is 24 degrees in here," Papa said. "We only serve hot treats to keep you toasty. Like Hit the Spot Hot Chocolate, Piping Pudding, and Molten Lava Cake!"

Each ice table had a centerpiece, an ice sculpture carved into an appropriate sugary con-fection. The walls and the counter where everything was prepared were also ice. Lights representing icicles hung from the ceiling. The showpiece of the room was the ice slide. Peter and Lina took turns going down it before they had to move on to the last room.

"This is the room you can warm up in," Papa said. "It is kept at 84 degrees and we only serve cold treats to keep you nice and cool."

This room had all the fixings of a charming summer's day at the park. Large sun-like ceiling lights circulated the warm air. The paved walkway led straight to a counter designed as part of an ice cream truck. There were picnic tables, real live trees and flower beds to add to the summertime feel of the whole place. In the center of the park there was a water fountain with an enormous ice cream sundae sculpted out of stone.

"This is so awesome! I can't believe it!" Peter exclaimed.

Papa winked. "You should be able to believe almost anything after the things you have seen, Peter. We better get downstairs now before Nana has to come looking for us."

Friends, family, kids from school, everyone from miles around must have come to the party. Peter was cheerless when it ended. He wanted the night to go on forever. Peter's excitement was rejuvenated when he remembered what would be happening at the end of his night.

Peter reached into his pocket and pulled out the angel figurine that Henry had given him before facing Goaltan. Peter had tried to return it to Mr. Rupert, but Mr. Rupert asked if it was alright if they made an even swap, Peter's soldier action figure for the figurine. Mr. Rupert said that the soldier added color to the collection and it was a nice reminder of the day his life changed for the better. He placed the angel carefully on top of the cash register. There it would remain.

It was time to go. Instead of heading toward the door, Papa headed toward the elevator and started walking with Nana. He looked back over his shoulder and said, "Come along, everyone. I want to show you something."

Peter and his family, Lina and her family, Mr. Rupert and his son and daughter-in-law all piled into the elevator. Papa took a key out of his pocket. Once the doors closed, he picked up the phone and said, "Home Sweet Home." A second later a small plaque that read "Emergency Phone" opened up like a mailbox and a keyhole appeared. Papa stuck his key inside and turned. *A secret room! What else could there be?* Peter thought.

When the doors opened, Peter recognized one thing immediately: Nana and Papa's floral couch. It was a home—Nana and Papa's home.

"Dad, what is this?" Peter's father inquired.

"Your mom and I thought it would be nice to close up shop and be home. I always thought of my sweet shop as my second home. Now it can truly be home. We sold our old house to a lovely young couple who are expecting twins." Papa smiled, slyly pointing to Buddy and Lisa who were smiling guiltily.

"Twins? Double grandtastic! I can't believe it! Y'all are sly ones." Mr. Rupert bent toward Lisa's pregnant belly and said to his grandbabies, "We are goin' to have loads of fun!"

It was finally time for what Peter had been eagerly awaiting all night, months actually. Nana saved her Honeyville story and promised to tell it in its full glory after the grand opening of Papa's Sweet Shop. She said it would make the night that much more special. At first, Peter didn't like the idea of waiting. After some consideration, he knew the anticipation of hearing Nana's story would be like waiting for his birthday. Tonight, the waiting was finally over and his biggest gift would be unwrapped.

Award-winning author **Crystal Marcos** has been a storyteller her entire life. Being the oldest of five children, she had a lot of entertaining to do. Crystal lives on the Kitsap Peninsula in Washington State with her husband and their daughter, Kaylee. Her first book, *BELLYACHE: A Delicious Tale*, won the Readers Favorite Silver Award in its category.

Visit her at www.CrystalMarcos.com

Made in the USA
Columbia, SC
28 November 2020